Nicholas Aaron Hodge

K. M. Lightfoot

A Horror Comic Anthology

Featuring

Mind Shattering!

ART BY
Wayne Oliver Lowdy
Joaquin Espinosa
Jesusa Diaz
Renato Zechetto

Eye Popping!

ADDITIONAL LETTERING BY
Marina Leon

Spine Chilling!

LITERATURE BY
John McDevitt
Sera Rae Young

Heart Stopping!

COVER ART BY
Frederik Hornung
Joaquin Espinosa

 @ComicsToYourCouch

Before We Begin...

We want to take a moment to appreciate the spectacular journey of making this book. This anthology was birthed almost exclusively from years of shared love and admiration for often maligned and forgotten cult horror media. Which only goes to show how important the preservation of physical media really is.

We also want to take a moment to recognize that this work would not have been possible without the combined talents of artists from around the world. All of which have worked earnestly to bring these bizarre, emotional, action-packed works of original fiction from two independent writers to life. A feat which is just as marvelous as the enduring myth of the Werewolf itself. We are eternally grateful to our collaborators and excited to share these stories with you.

From the inception of this anthology, we endeavored to create unique worlds and characters for stories that challenged the traditional expectations and structure of the classically constructed Werewolf story. We wanted to create stories that attempted to bring the Werewolf into the modern context of the world. Tales that created new and lasting fans for the classic sub-horror genre we love most.

We have been telling stories all our lives, but it feels especially important in the modern world to make the effort to strive to create lasting visions and records of beliefs in a better world. Testaments to the beauty of life despite all of its struggles and flaws; persisting nonetheless, with wild, hopeful abandon, much like our titular beast.

We hope you enjoy the following tales and endeavor to share them with a friend, family member, or loved one who would delight in the kind of imaginative, fantastic, emotionally gripping, impactful storytelling that only the horror genre can deliver!

Nicholas Aaron Hodge

K.M. Lightfoot

Published By:
ComicsToYourCouch

Written and Edited By:
Nicholas Aaron Hodge
& Kaleb M. Lightfoot

Cover Art By:
Joaquin Espinosa
Frederik Hornung

Interior Art By:
Wayne Oliver Lowdy
Jesusa Diaz
Joaquin Espinosa
Renato Zecchetto

Contributors:
Sera Young
John McDevitt

Lettering BY:
Marina Leon

TABLE OF CONTENTS

A Dying Breed

Written by
Nicholas Aaron Hodge

Art by
Wayne Oliver Lowdy

Lettering by
Marina Leon

A DYING BREED

Written by
NICHOLAS AARON
HODGE

Art by
WAYNE OLIVER
LOWDY

Letters by
MARINA
LEON

I spend most of my nights half asleep. Some primal part of me awake and listening--

Waiting all this time to hear-- I don't know what. An answer maybe? A reason for it all.

I know I'm not alone. A lot of people come out here looking for answers--

But after all these years, I just keep coming back with more questions...

FIRST AID

HERE WE ARE MY DEAR-- JUST THE WAY YOU LIKE IT...
THANK YOU, CAROL ANN.
I've been coming to this place for thirty seven seasons...
HOWDY, CAN WE GET A TABLE FOR FOUR?
THIS PLACE LOOKS DISGUSTING...
OH COME ON BABE, THIS IS WHERE THE REAL TRAVELERS GO--
A place like this has a lot in common with a Forest...
MAYBE WE SHOULD POP AN INTRO FOR THE VIDEO REAL QUICK...
HERE?
YEAH WHY NOT? IT'S AUTHENTIC.
Consistent. Slow to change, but growing ever still.

SUP, IT'S YOUR BOY TATE FROM "TATESTRAILTRIALS", WITH THE CREW-- MY BOY KYLER, BEST HUNTER IN THE BIZ--
Neither good nor bad just-- here.
LEVS, THE SURVIVAL KING, AND MY GIRL ADDIYSON FOR STANDING AROUND AND YAPPIN'--
Maybe it's foolish to love something like that...
REAL FUNNY TATE--
BUT IT'S TIME TO GET SERIOUS, CAUSE THIS WEEK WE'RE VENTURING INTO THE "MOST DANGEROUS NATIONAL PARK" WITH OVER 100 DEATHS AND 300 DISAPPEARANCES IN THE LAST 50 YEARS!
THE NORTH CASCADES...
WERE-- WERE Y'ALL READY TO ORDER NOW?
ACTUALLY, I WANTED TO ASK A LOCAL IF YOU KNEW ANYONE IN TOWN WHO'D CAMPED OUT THERE?
WE HEARD IT'S LIKE SUPER DANGEROUS, RIGHT?

YEAH... PEOPLE GO MISSING ALL THE TIME--
SORRY, I-- I DON'T REALLY LIKE BEING FILMED. AND YOUR FRIEND CAN'T SMOKE IN HERE...
ALRIGHT, PUT THE CAMERA DOWN, BABE-- I THINK WE'RE SCARING THE LOCALS.
DON'T DO IT...
DON'T GO UP THERE.
IT'S PROHIBITED BY FEDERAL LAW FOR ANY INDIVIDUAL TO SET ONE FOOT IN THOSE WOODS AND MORE IMPORTANTLY, YOU'D BE RISKING YOUR LIVES.
THE HELL?
PSSHH-- WHAT DO YOU KNOW, OLD MAN?
I'VE BEEN A FOREST RANGER IN THESE PARTS LONGER THAN ANY OF YOU HAVE BEEN ALIVE... WHICH MEANS I AM THE ONE THAT FINDS THE BODIES.
MENU

IT DOESN'T MATTER HOW STRONG YOU THINK YOU ARE-- HOW PREPARED YOU MIGHT BE...
SOME THINGS IN THIS WORLD ARE BEST LEFT ALONE.
SLAM
WHO THE FUCK DO YOU THINK YOU'RE TALKING TO?!
YOU DON'T KNOW SHIT ABOUT ME!
AH MAN, I WAS HUNGRY...
THESE PEOPLE DON'T DESERVE OUR MONEY.
Y'ALL BETTER MIND YOUR FUCKIN' BUSINESS--
It's like I'm stuck somewhere, rooted in the past.
Sometimes, I wonder if I'm still part of the same world.

SORRY ABOUT THAT EVERETT...
NOT YOUR FAULT. KEEP THE CHANGE.
Truth is-- the world is the same, it's just been cut into smaller and smaller pieces. Which is why it's so important to protect my piece--
SCREECH
Pretty soon, I'll be gone. I've already decided. This is my last season.
CAN'T BELIEVE THAT WRINKLY DUDE WAS TRYING TO INTIMIDATE US--
HE'S WORRIED PEOPLE ARE GONNA FIND HIM DOIN SOME FREAKY SHIT OUT THERE...
GOOGLE SAYS IT IS TECHNICALLY ILLEGAL TO CAMP CAUSE OF TREE PRESERVATION OR WHATEV- WAIT... IS THAT HIM BEHIND US?
PSYCHO...
THINK HE TOOK YOUR PLATES?
WHATEVER BRO, LET'S FINISH THAT INTRO--
WILL THE CASCADES FINALLY CONQUER OUR CREW? SMASH THAT LIKE BUTTON AND SUBSCRIBE TO FIND OUT!

We do our best to ignore it, but life is far more strange than we realize. So before you step into the unknown...
GODDAMNIT...
I WARNED 'EM, DIDN'T I?
...you better have a good reason.

YOU GOT THIS BRO--
WHOOOO!
BANG
CRASH
YO! WHAT THE FUCK?!
YOU SCARED THE SHIT OUT OF ME--
CALM DOWN MAN, I KNOW WHAT I'M--
YOU REALLY THINK THAT THE WHOLE WORLD BELONGS TO YOU, DON'T YOU?
HEY-- WHO IS THAT?!
YOU CAN'T IMAGINE A REALITY WHERE YOU CAN'T TAKE EXACTLY WHAT YOU WANT...

WHAT ARE YOU GONNA DO, YOU OLD BITCH?
WAIT-- IS HE GETTING NAKED?
I'M GONNA GIVE YOU TEN MINUTES TO PACK UP AND GO. THAT'S GENEROUS.
AFTER THAT-- I CAN'T HELP YOU ANYMORE.
BABY WAIT-- LET'S JUST GO!
HE'S RUINING OUR WHOLE TRIP!
HE AIN'T A COP-- I'M NOT GOING ANYWHERE.
DID-- DID HE LOOK KINDA DIFFERENT?
AARROOOOoo
WHAT THE ACTUAL FUCK?!
SHOULD WE LIKE... CHECK ON HIM?
WHAT? WHY?!
I DON'T KNOW! MAYBE HE FELL. HE'S SO OLD...

HEY-- IF ANYBODY COMES ASKING, I DIDN'T SEE SH--
SHHHH! QUIET. SOMETHING'S BACK THERE.
YOU DON'T GOTTA DO THE WHOLE "HUNTER" THING WHEN WE AREN'T FILMING, DUDE.
OH SHIT-- MAYBE WE SHOULD BE FILMING...
I'M GONNA CHECK IT OUT.
NO, ADDY-- DON'T!
HELLO? WHOA, IT'S SO QUIET...
WHERE'D ALL THE ANIMALS GO?
YO, WHAT YOU CALLIN' HER "ADDY" FOR BRO?
GUYS, I DON'T SEE...
...ANYTHING...

GHHRRnnn
FUCK THIS!
WHATEVER IT IS, I'M KILLING IT!
HE WAS SUPPOSED TO BE A SURVIVAL EXPERT...
BANG BANG BANG
I KNOW YOU'RE THERE... YOU CAN'T HIDE FROM ME.
KY?! BRO, STOP! FUCK!
WHAT IS GOING ON?!
SHHRKHHHHHE
I GOTTA-- I GOTTA GET HELP...

BABE, WHAT THE HELL HAPPENED?!
MAN, WE GOTTA GO!
TALK TO ME, ARE YOU HURT?
SHE COULD BE IN SHOCK...
BE-BEH-- BEHIND--
HOLY FUCK!
LEVS?! WHAT IS--
WE-WE GOTTA GET HIM OUT!
YAAAARGHH!

GRRrrr
YO, IF ANY OF MY FOLLOWERS ARE IN THE AREA...
SOME CRAZY SHIT IS GOING DOWN OUT IN THIS FOREST AND--
H-HELLO? ADDIYSON?
GRRAH!
AAAHHRH

MORNING, EVERETT!
BUSY NIGHT?
HOW YA FEELING?
SORE.
YOU MISSED ONE YOU KNOW...
AW HELL BOB, I'M SORRY...
NEVER YOU MIND, IT'S OKAY... I TOOK CARE OF IT.
DID YOU NOW?

H-HEELLLLPP MEEEE...
OH, I'D LIKE TO SON, BUT I'VE KNOWN EVERETT FOR MORE THAN A FEW DECADES NOW--
SO I KNOW THAT HE MUST'VE GIVEN YOU FOLKS PLENTY OF WARNINGS--
PLEASE.
Y'ALL JUST DIDN'T LISTEN.
SPLRTCH

I TOLD YOU I WAS GETTING SLOW. CARELESS.

YOU'RE THE BEST RANGER THIS PARK HAS EVER HAD, THAT'S ALL THAT MATTERS.

SURE.
I JUST HOPE THAT'S ENOUGH...
END....?

MANY MOONS

A COMPENDIUM OF WEREWOLF EPISODES OF ANTHOLOGY TELEVISION | BY JOHN MCDEVITT OF SUPER-HORROR-RAMA!

As night falls, you turn off the lights and switch on the TV. It glows like the full moon. You feel its gravitational pull. The room pulsates with artificial light. You watch as shapes dart across the screen. Your heart beats faster. Your imagination runs wild. You are transformed.

The book in your hands (or blood-soaked paws) sniffs out monsters of a particular breed—thick pelt, huge teeth, and a craving for fresh meat. As enduring as the werewolf is in pop culture, it appears infrequently in horror anthology television—most series of this type have only one werewolf episode or none—but chances are you're in for a treat when a pack, lone wolf, or cub claim their territory.

The episodes listed here are from over thirty series around the world and across time, 1960 to the present day. Many stand out for their quality or connection to well-known talent, and every episode is worth watching as a new perspective on werewolves. Serialized television and docuseries are excluded to maintain focus on

stand-alone and make-believe tales with a werewolf as the main antagonist—or protagonist! The lore is merely teased in the first entry, "The Howling Man" from *The Twilight Zone*, and a few later entries save werewolf identities for a hairy surprise at the end.

Get ready for horror anthology heavy hitters like *Tales from the Darkside* (1983-1988) and *Tales from the Crypt* (1989-1996), animated series like *Tales from the Cryptkeeper* (1993-1999) and *Love, Death & Robots* (2019-present), go-to children's programming like *Are You Afraid of the Dark?* (1991-1996) and *Goosebumps* (1995-1998), fiction/nonfiction hybrids like *Beyond Belief: Fact or Fiction* (1997-2002) and *Lost Tapes* (2008-2010), less horror-oriented shows like *Love, American Style* (1969-1974) and *Fantasy Island* (1977-1984), and streaming originals like *Into the Dark* (2018-2021) and *Creepshow* (2019-2023).

All episodes are listed in order of their original broadcast date and rated on a four-moon scale. Four moons activate the full power of the beast! Additional notes highlight source material, other media with the same cast and crew, and wolf-centric honorable mentions.

You're ravenous. The drool dangles from your chin. The chain that holds you grows taught—it snaps! You crash through the wall, blaze through the night, and follow your snout to the feast ahead. You spot your prey, and the feeding frenzy begins! You slam down your paws. You sink in your teeth. You tear away the flesh. Now don't stop until you devour every last bone....

🌑🌑🌑🌑
"The Howling Man"
The Twilight Zone
Season 2, Episode 5
November 4, 1960

"When I told you that no man howled at the hermitage, I was being perfectly honest. What you saw is not a man."

While not a werewolf story, this episode certainly evokes the lore.

A man on a walking trip in Central Europe loses his way in a storm and begs for shelter at a creepy castle lit with torches. The monks inside refuse his stay until he collapses from exhaustion. When he awakens, he follows an unearthly howling to a cell where a man in tattered garb says the monks are madmen. The leader of the order (John Carradine) claims the prisoner is the devil himself!

Episode director Douglas Heyes was inspired by *Werewolf of London* (1935) when envisioning the transformation sequence for the devil. Utilizing hidden cuts as the character strides behind a series of columns, he reappears each time in creepier makeup.

🌑🌑🌑🌑
"The Phantom Farmhouse"
Night Gallery
Season 2, Episode 5
October 20, 1971

"Men of science say miracles are past and give reasons for things supernatural. Therefore, we dismiss our terror by finding safety in false knowledge when instead we should submit ourselves to an unknown fear."

This gothic romance gives us monsters of a unique crossbreed: werewolf ghosts! A psychiatrist (David McCallum) visits a countryside sanitarium and investigates the strange claims of a patient (David Carradine) with pentagrams on his palms. The giveaways for werewolves in this eerie, dreamlike tale are bright red nails, an index finger longer than the middle finger, and eyes that turn red at moonrise.

Based on a short story by Seabury Quinn that originally appeared in *Weird Tales* (October 1923), this episode is directed by French filmmaker Jeannot Szwarc, who later gave us natural horror films *Bug* (1975) and *Jaws 2* (1978).

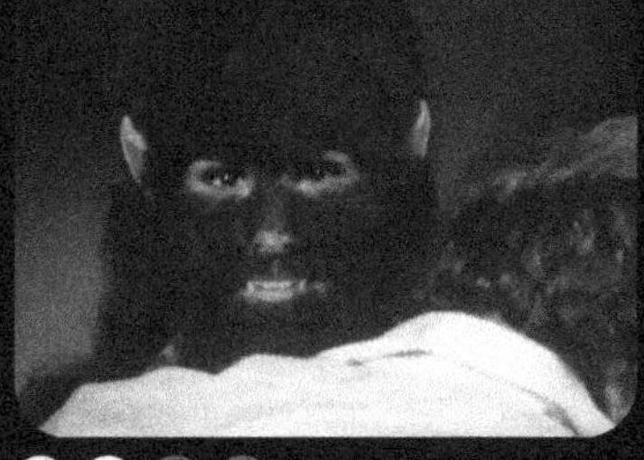

⬤ ⬤ ⬤ ⬤

"Love and the Hairy Excuse"
Love, American Style
Season 4, Episode 9
November 10, 1972

"Well, my love, it's one thing to borrow a lawnmower from your next-door neighbor, but it's quite another thing to eat his face."

This shrill slapstick comedy is about a cheating husband who lies about being a werewolf to explain to his wife why he stays out so late. What he doesn't know is that *she* is a werewolf!

The cast must be praised for their total commitment to the absurd. Episode writer Ron Friedman previously wrote for *Bewitched* (1964-1972) and *I Dream of Jeannie* (1965-1970), and "Hairy Excuse" plays like a backdoor pilot for another supernatural sitcom.

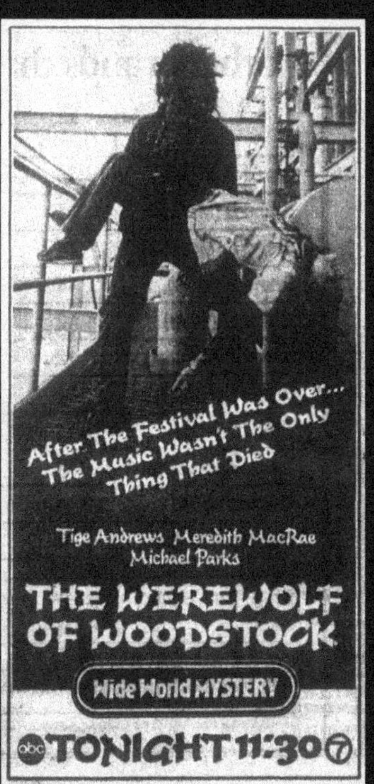

⬤ ⬤ ⬤ ⬤

"The Werewolf of Woodstock"
The Wide World of Mystery
Season 3, Episode 22
January 24, 1975

"Oh, excuse *me*! This is 1969, and this is a modern *electrical* werewolf!"

After the first Woodstock music

festival, a cranky farmer tries to demolish the empty stage. He grabs a live wire, the electrical current alters his body at the molecular level, and he transforms into a violent beast that attacks people in the night. Authorities assume the long-haired killer is a crazed hippie until the evidence points to an honest-to-goodness werewolf. The police team up with psychedelic rockers to lure the music-hating creature out of hiding, but then it uses a dune buggy as a getaway vehicle!

Filmed on videotape, this is a campy, charming descendent of early monster movies in all their pseudoscientific glory. Makeup artist Joe Blasco worked on David Cronenberg's first widely released features, *Shivers* (1975) and *Rabid* (1977). He was also the personal makeup artist for many Hollywood stars including Marlene Dietrich and Orson Welles, and he taught makeup to Kim Kardashian.

⬤ ⬤ ⬤ ⬤

"What Big Eyes"
Beasts
Season 1, Episode 5
November 13, 1976

"Don't you see it wasn't the wolf that swallowed grandma? Grandma was the wolf. Pure lycanthropy. A folk memory."

An RSPCA inspector questions the records of an animal dealer listing a pet shop as the shipping destination for Hungarian timber wolves. The shop clerk is a timid middle-aged woman, and her father is a grizzled animal trainer (the ever wild-eyed Patrick Magee) who sees flaws in Darwin's theory of evolution and believes the real answers are found in lycanthropy.

This heart-wrenching fable is written by Nigel Kneale of *The Quatermass Experiment* (1953), *The Stone Tape* (1972), and *The Woman in Black* (1989). He was also the screenwriter behind Hammer Film Productions' *The Abominable Snowman* (1957) and *The Witches* (1966), and he wrote the original screenplay for *Halloween III: Season of the Witch* (1982) before it was passed along to Tommy Lee Wallace.

⬤ ⬤ ⬤ ⬤

**"Countess Ilona"
& "The Werewolf Reunion"**
Supernatural
Season 1, Episodes 2 & 3
June 18 & 25, 1977

"You didn't know that like so many of our betters, he had running through his veins what the gypsies call...bad blood?"

1880: A widowed Countess hosts four guests at her Transylvanian castle shrouded in mist. These past lovers (from her days as a courtesan) arranged her meeting with the Count, an abusive man who believed he was suffering from lycanthropy before his untimely death. Any of these men could be the father of her son, a strange boy who dreams of wolves and fancies candied fruit.

This is the only two-part episode of *Supernatural*. Billie Whitelaw, who played the evil nanny in *The Omen* (1976), exudes dignity and strength as the Countess, and one of her guests is played by Ian Hendry, who appeared in many classics of British horror including *Children of the Damned* (1964), *Tales from The Crypt* (1972), and *Theatre of Blood* (1973).

⬤ ⬤ ⬤ ⬤

"Children of the Full Moon"
Hammer House of Horror
Season 1, Episode 8
November 1, 1980

"...they live in packs, wolves do. And each pack has its leader. And the leader has many mates and many cubs."

After a near-fatal car crash, a pair of honeymooners find themselves stranded at a mysterious manor full of children, "cheeky little pups" as their mother calls them. After a hellish overnight stay, the husband wakes up in hospital and

thinks it was all a dream...until the next road trip gives him *déjà vu*.

This scatterbrained episode was scripted by Murray Smith, a prolific writer of television crime dramas who also wrote horror and exploitation films for cult filmmaker Pete Walker. *Hammer House of Horror* was produced by Hammer Film Productions, whose only werewolf movie was *The Curse of the Werewolf* (1961).

⬤ ⬤ ⬤ ⬤

"Gabriel-Ernest"
Spine Chillers
Season 1, Episode 15
December 11, 1980

"...he wished the boy had not made that uncanny remark about childflesh eaten two months ago. Such dreadful things should not be said even in fun."

Spine Chillers was a short-lived all-horror offshoot of *Jackanory* (1965-1996), a British children's series in which actors read aloud children's stories, a transatlantic precursor to *Reading Rainbow*. Jonathan Pryce appeared in five episodes of the series to read stories by Saki including this one about a feral child. Pryce later played a killer disguised as a werewolf in comedy horror classic *Haunted Honeymoon* (1986).

⬤ ⬤ ⬤ ⬤

"Man-Beast"
Fantasy Island
Season 4, Episode 23
May 16, 1981

"I love you so much that what I'm doing to you rips at my guts even more than that thing that happens to me at night."

A married man (David Hedison) is tormented by nightmares about his wife in peril. When they ask for help at Fantasy Island, the man transforms into a werewolf, and the only cure is a rare orchid that draws its life from the moon.

David Hedison appeared in six episodes of *Fantasy Island* and was known for another beastly metamorphosis in *The Fly* (1958). He also starred in *Voyage to the Bottom of the Sea* (1964-1968), which had an episode called "Man-Beast" (February 18, 1968) in which his character transformed into a werewolf-like creature.

"The Bogeyman Will Get You"
Darkroom
Season 1, Episode 2
December 4, 1981

"I know what you think...that I'm crazy. But he scares me. There's something about him!"

On their way home from a monster movie at the drive-in, two teenage sisters nearly hit someone on the road. Turns out he's a family friend who's staying in a cabin across the lake to work on his thesis about demonology in the modern world. The little sister thinks he's a vampire, and the big sister (Helen Hunt) finds him irresistible.

Originally broadcast the same year *The Howling* and *An American Werewolf in London* were released in theaters, this episode is based on a short story by Robert Bloch (*Psycho*) that originally appeared in *Weird Tales* (March 1946).

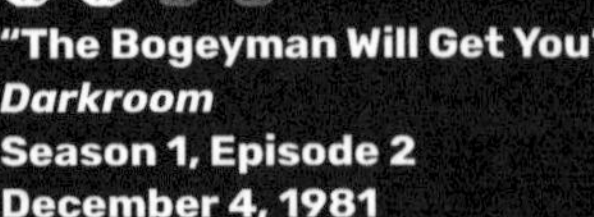

"The Adventures of a Two-Minute Werewolf"
ABC Weekend Specials
Season 8, Episodes 4 & 5
February 23 & March 2, 1985

"They're not gonna put you in prison. In the zoo, maybe."

A boy celebrates his thirteenth birthday by going to see his favorite movie, *The Wolf Man*

(1941). He discovers on his walk home that he's a wolf-boy who randomly transforms for two minutes at a time. He fights crime, comes out to his parents, and discovers Mom has a secret, too.

Based on a 1983 chapter book by Gene DeWeese (best known for his *Star Trek* novels) and full of canine and lupine puns, this is the first produced screenplay of Pamela Pettler, co-writer of *Corpse Bride* (2005) and *Monster House* (2006).

"Family Reunion"
Tales from the Darkside
Season 4, Episode 16
May 22, 1988

"I feel wild and crazy and really strong like I could do anything!"

A father (Stephen McHattie) keeps his son in hiding because the boy is a werewolf who's becoming increasingly out of control. The mother (Patricia Tallman) recruits a social worker to help rescue the boy. For his final transformation, he creeps across his room and emerges from every shadow looking more like a monster. It's easy to guess the twist (that the mother is a werewolf, too), but it leads to a surprisingly sentimental conclusion as wolf-mother and wolf-son embrace in slow motion and give each other love licks.

This is the last of three *Darkside* episodes directed by Tom Savini. Tallman reunited with Savini to play Barbara in his 1990 remake of *Night of the Living Dead*. "Family Reunion" is the tenth and final *Darkside* episode written by Edithe Swensen, who wrote early scripts for *Charmed* (1998-2006).

"Red Smoke in the Veins"
The Marked Hour
1989

"A murder of that nature isn't something to take lightly when you could be the next victim."

A killer is on the loose! Is it a wild beast that escaped from the zoo? A psychopath? A monster? Raúl suffers from an unknown illness, and his devoted wife Susana does everything she can to help. When their friend Laura tries to seduce Raúl, Susana moves her weekly gal pal gathering to the night of the full moon and arranges for Laura to be left alone with Raúl.

A "Woman in Black" appears in this episode and throughout the series as a personification of death. The show helped launch the careers of Mexican filmmakers like Guillermo del Toro and Alfonso Cuarón, who each wrote multiple episodes.

"Conjugal Conflict"
The Marked Hour
1990

"...it would hurt me to turn such a good friend as him into my dinner."

A timid man tries to please his wife on every special occasion from their wedding anniversary to her birthday, but all she does is berate him. When he discovers the local werewolf is his friendly next-door neighbor, it's time to ask a favor.

"One Wolf's Family"
Monsters
Season 2, Episode 17
February 11, 1990

"I will not have a were-hyena for a son-in-law!"

A werewolf immigrant celebrates America as a place where everyone is welcome. He doesn't see the irony in his prejudice against his daughter's fiancé, a laughing were-hyena. Meanwhile, nosy neighbor Mrs. Peabody peeks

---

through the window and is aghast to see monsters feasting on dismembered human bodies!

This episode follows in the footsteps of bizarro family sitcoms like *Small Wonder* (1985-1989) and *Alf* (1986-1990). The father and his wife are played by real-life couple Jerry Stiller and Anne Meara, and the daughter is played by one of their real-life offspring, Amy Stiller (Ben Stiller's sister). Episode writer Paul Dini is one of the visionaries behind the DC Animated Universe.

"The Secret"
Tales from the Crypt
Season 2, Episode 18
July 31, 1990

"Now here is a story you can sink your *teeth* into, a toothsome tale of tommyrot guaranteed to scare the *dickens* out of you."

Theodore is an orphan in a coonskin cap who wonders about his real parents. He's adopted by the Colberts, a wealthy couple who lock him in his room all day every day with an endless supply of toys and sweets. Theo's only friend is the butler, who defies the heads of the household to save the boy from a terrible fate.

This second-season finale is faithful to the original story from *The Haunt of Fear, No. 24* (1954) and adds quite a bit of heart in the form of the butler played by Larry Drake (*Darkman*). Mrs. Colbert is played with glamour and menace by Grace Zabriskie (*Twin Peaks*).

"Werewolf of Hollywood"
Monsters
Season 3, Episode 20
February 10, 1991

"Here's a counteroffer. I'll rip out your throat and throw your body down the canyon!"

A sardonic screenwriter (Richard Belzer) and his new assistant are assigned to a film about a wolf who rose through the ranks in the film industry, but is the producer's outline based on a true story?

This goofy Hollywood satire is written by Ron Goulart, based on his short story of the same name from *Pulphouse: The Hardback Magazine, No. 3* (1989), during his collaboration with William Shatner on the *TekWar* franchise.

"Werewolf Concerto"
Tales from the Crypt
Season 4, Episode 13
September 9, 1992

"That whole hair-on-the-back thing's always been a big turnoff for me."

The guests at a luxury resort are informed that one of them is a werewolf and another hunts werewolves, and nobody knows who's who. Told from the point of view of the werewolf (Timothy Dalton), he navigates red herrings in a game for his life and still finds time to flirt with a *femme fatale* concert pianist (Beverly D'Angelo).

This old-fashioned whodunnit is faithful to the twist at the end of the original story in *The Vault of Horror, No. 16* (1950) and comedically revamps the rest for the modern era. There's even a cameo appearance by celebrity chef Wolfgang Puck because why not when his name is so on point?

"The Tale of the Full Moon"
Are You Afraid of the Dark?
Season 2, Episode 9
August 21, 1993

"There's lots of different kinds of families, Jed. This is just one of them."

Jed is a young pet detective living in a pastel suburb like the one in *Edward Scissorhands* (1990). He grows suspicious of a neighbor in a fortified house with a fridge full of raw meat. After Jed catches the man turning into a wolf, Mom invites the monster to dinner!

Episode writer-director Ron Oliver worked frequently on this series, *Goosebumps* (1995-1998), and *The Nightmare Room* (2001-2002).

Honorable mention to "The Tale of the Hunted" (March 27, 1999), an episode of *Are You Afraid of the Dark?*'s first revival, in which a girl from a hunting family morphs into an ordinary wolf and learns what it's like to walk in those paws.

"Hyde and Go Shriek"
Tales from the Cryptkeeper
Season 1, Episode 8
November 6, 1993

"Guaranteed to turn even the scrawniest dweeb into a bloodthirsty battling beast overnight!"

Class nerd Wendell doesn't mind that muscle-bound Rex picks on him until the bully crashes show-and-tell and loses Wendell's pet rat, Dr. Jekyll. A stoner-coded classmate sells Wendell a magic root tea that makes you grow muscle in a matter of days, but it turns him into a werewolf. Now law enforcement are after him, and they've got a tranquilizer gun!

Episode director Laura Shepherd previously worked on animated tie-ins for some of the weirdest toys of the '80s, Madballs and My Pet Monster, and episode writer Dana Olsen previously scripted Joe Dante's *The 'Burbs* (1989) and John Carpenter's *Memoirs of an Invisible Man* (1992).

Cryptkeeper's second season gave

---

us "Hunted" (November 19, 1994), a werewolf-adjacent tale of a hairy bipedal beast that hunts down poachers in the Amazon.

"The Werewolf of Fever Swamp"
Goosebumps
Season 1, Episodes 18 & 19
March 11, 1996

"People usually don't move into Fever Swamp. They move out."

Grady and his big sister move to the swamp so their parents can study a herd of deer adapting to a new environment. It's hard for the kids to adapt, too, when their new house has no TV reception and the local boy in overalls keeps saying the town hermit is a werewolf.

This two-part first-season finale is filmed mostly at night through branches and fog. Along the way, you'll see a bog that swallows you whole like quicksand, thrilling chase sequences shot from the monster's point of view, and a well-timed lunar eclipse that de-morphs the creature enough to reveal its true identity!

Episode director William Fruet previously made numerous horror films for adults like *Spasms* (1983) and *Killer Party* (1986). *Fever Swamp* was later adapted by Eisner Award winner Gabriel Hernández Walta for the first *Goosebumps* comic anthology, *Creepy Creatures* (2006).

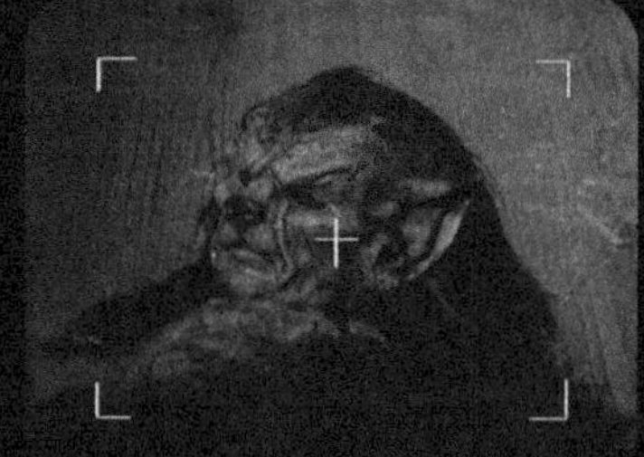

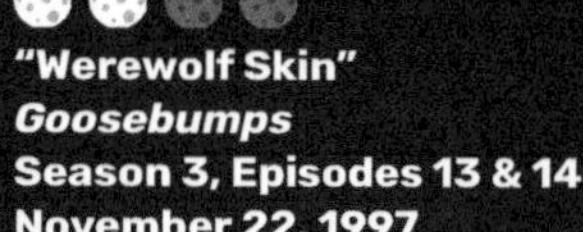

"Werewolf Skin"
Goosebumps
Season 3, Episodes 13 & 14
November 22, 1997

"What really happens is when the sun rises the werewolf sheds its skin, and if someone finds that skin and destroys it before the next full moon is at its highest point the curse is over and the werewolf inside the person dies."

An aspiring photographer goes to stay with his aunt and uncle in the small town of Wolf Creek. He looks for creepy pictures to take for a contest ("first prize is a thousand bucks") and sets his sights on a run-down house across the street.

Ron Oliver is back in the director's chair with another werewolf story for kids, adapting a *Goosebumps* book published just two months prior. He also directed wolf-centric two-parter "Welcome to Camp Nightmare" (November 17 & 24, 1995) about campers terrorized by a giant beast named Sabre.

"Eclipse"
Beyond Belief: Fact or Fiction
Season 3, Episode 6
June 30, 2000

"Life is still precious, even to a werewolf."

A disgraced history professor recounts how he ended up in a padded cell. Ever since he was attacked by a wolf in Romania, he experienced violent blackouts during every full moon. Convinced that he's a werewolf, he dreads the warning he read in a monastic text that all of the werewolves of the world will die during the total eclipse of the full moon if they are exposed to it. He begs to be moved to a windowless cell, but will the powers that be allow it?

Every episode of *Beyond Belief* contains five stories. The viewer is challenged to guess which are fact and which are fiction before all the answers are revealed at the end. "Eclipse" is just "crying wolf," and it's written and directed by Tony Randel, who previously directed *Hellbound: Hellraiser II* (1988) and *Ticks* (1993).

The German-produced revival of the series featured a werewolf segment called "Candle in the Woods" in the premiere episode broadcast on Halloween, 2021.

"Cry Wolf"
Urban Gothic
Season 1, Episode 8
July 12, 2000

"Brings a whole new meaning to doing it doggy style."

Ex-lovers working for law enforcement as an inspector and a WPC (Woman Police Constable) team up to investigate the case of a feral man they found gnawing on human remains in a nest of old celluloid at an abandoned cinema. Turns out the wild man is part wolf, and the constable grows strangely fond of him, which makes the inspector jealous. Many secrets come to light by episode's end including a pack of feral children left behind at the theater.

"Full Moon Halloween"
The Nightmare Room
Season 1, Episode 7
October 27, 2001

"I'll tell you what the deal is. One of you knows firsthand about those animal attacks. One of you is the werewolf. And we're not leaving this house until it's destroyed."

Spooky pop-up cards invite five friends to a Halloween party at an unfamiliar house when the moon is full. When they arrive, one of them reveals it's *his* house, and he intends to expose one of the others as a werewolf. The doors are locked, the windows are barred, and the big crate in the living room contains fuzzy creatures called "plogs," which are werewolf hunters that look like *Star Trek*'s tribbles—if they had red eyes and sharp teeth!

This episode is a loose adaptation of *Full Moon Halloween* (2001), the tenth installment in R. L. Stine's book series *The Nightmare Room*, in which a deranged teacher and his wife are the hosts of the party.

"Something with Bite"
Fear Itself
Season 1, Episode 9
January 3, 2009

"We're gonna need a bigger gurney."

Wilbur is an apathetic husband, father, and veterinarian who finds his life turned upside down when an injured wolf-like creature (with pierced ears and a gold filling) turns up at the clinic and chomps on his arm. Wilbur becomes a werewolf with heightened senses and a renewed zest for life, but a serial killer dubbed "The Beast" seems to target everyone in Wilbur's inner circle. Is Wilbur the killer, or is it a werewolf wannabe?

This episode is directed by Ernest Dickerson (*Demon Knight*) and written by Max Landis, son of John Landis (*An American Werewolf in London*). Episode star Wendell Pierce was the first actor to be cast for *The Wire* (2002-2008) and was in the main cast of that series for all five seasons.

"Werewolf"
Lost Tapes
Season 2, Episode 4
October 13, 2009

"There's a dark underbelly to human nature that both attracts us and repels us."

A documentarian films the lead detectives on the case of a serial killer whose victims are scratched and bitten with traces of human and animal DNA. When the prime suspect brings home a date, the investigators hear a bloodcurdling scream, so they break down the door, search the house, and find the date wounded and whimpering in the basement.

Originally broadcast on Animal Planet, *Lost Tapes* is a found footage horror series that intercuts fictional narratives with real-life expert interviews. Topics discussed in this episode include the social structure of wolves, metamorphosis in the natural world, the lunar effect theory, and hypertrichosis. One of the talking heads is Rosemary Ellen Guiley, author of *The Encyclopedia of Vampires, Werewolves, and Other Monsters* (2004).

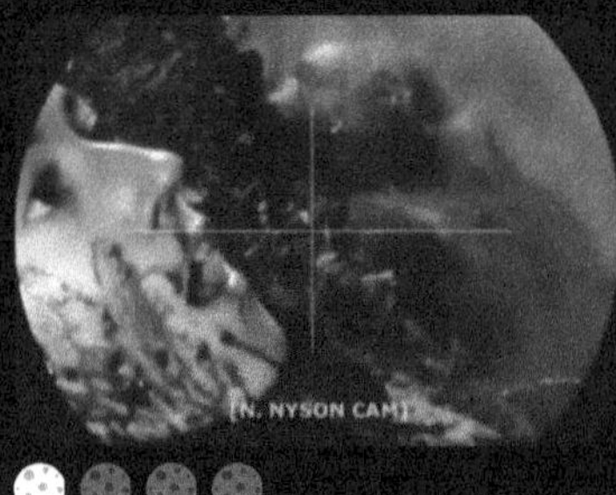

"Beast of Bray Road"
Lost Tapes
Season 3, Episode 9
November 2, 2010

"Not sure by who or by what, but we are *definitely* under attack."

A militia group think the Feds are after them until they see the attacker: a creature that walks on all fours! The urban legend of the Wisconsin Werewolf also inspired direct-to-video movie *The Beast of Bray Road* (2005) from The Asylum, the independent film studio that produced *Sharknado* (2013) and its many sequels.

"Nightmare Inn"
The Haunting Hour
Season 1, Episode 5
January 8, 2011

"Mom, I'm trying to escape my nightmares, not move into them."

A year after losing her father in a car accident, a teenage girl and her mother go to the Knight Time Inn—where Mom and Dad had their first Sunday brunch—so Mom can buy the business and fulfill a lifelong dream. The daughter has recurring nightmares about a werewolf that lurks on the grounds, and someone at the inn steals the last gift from her father, a silver necklace stamped with a message she'll soon understand.

Based a short story from R. L. Stine's *The Nightmare Hour* (1999), this adaptation builds on the original premise to create a much more complex, heartfelt, and satisfying narrative.

"Bite"
Twisted Tales
Season 1, Episode 5
March 1, 2013

"Yeah, I just bashed in the head of a friend after he chewed on another good buddy, and I'm just peachy keen."

In this slapdash stoner comedy, five twenty-somethings try a new designer drug called Bite (with a cartoon werewolf on the label), which is rumored to give people prophetic hallucinations. When they hear gunfire and turn on the news, the footage shows a sudden outbreak of werewolves. Is it real, a hoax, mass psychosis, or a vision of what *could* be?

Twisted Tales was a web series presented by video-on-demand service and cable channel Fearnet (2006-2014). Series creator Tom Holland previously gave us *Fright Night* (1985), which explored a vampire's ability to transform into a wolf, and *Child's Play* (1988). Shortly after appearing in "Bite," Ryan Kelley joined the cast of *Teen Wolf* to play a Hellhound for the series' final four seasons.

October 10, 2013, Nickelodeon's *Deadtime Stories* presented "The Beast of Baskerville," a spin on Sir Arthur Conan Doyle's hell-hound mystery, and it shows how a were-ram celebrates its birthday.

🔘🔘🔘⚪

"Face in the Car Lot"
Bobcat Goldthwait's Misfits & Monsters
Season 1, Episode 2
July 18, 2018

"I need to know if there's anything in your past that can bite us in the ass on the campaign."

Set in the 1970s, a used car salesman with no political experience runs for President of the United States, and a cub reporter exposes the skeezy candidate as a werewolf.

Inspired by the 2016 election, this biting satire guest stars sketch comedy legends David Koechner (*Saturday Night Live*) and Dave Foley (*The Kids in the Hall*). Series creator Bobcat Goldthwait previously voiced the Big Bad Wolf in "The Third Pig" (July 19, 1996), the animated series finale of *Tales from the Crypt*.

🔘🔘◐⚪

"Shape-Shifters"
Love, Death & Robots
Season 1, Episode 10
March 15, 2019

"No disrespect, Sergeant, but if you call us dog soldiers again I'll rip your arm off and beat you to death with it."

Created using motion capture and set in Afghanistan, werewolves from the U.S. Marine Corps and the Taliban battle in extremely gory detail in this tale of military machismo, tender brotherhood, racism against werewolf-kind, and ambivalence about war and the so-called civilized world.

Director Gabriele Pennacchioli began his animation career on wolf-centered *Balto* (1995) and worked on many other animated features about talking animals including *Kung Fu Panda* (2008).

🔘🔘🔘⚪

"Bad Wolf Down"
Creepshow
Season 1, Episode 2
October 3, 2019

"It's like you said, Sergeant. War changes a man."

During WWII, a Nazi officer (Jeffrey Combs) seeks revenge for his son's death and corners an American platoon in an abandoned police station. One of the cells holds a French woman who happens to be a werewolf, and she equips the soldiers to tear their enemy to shreds.

Episode writer-director Rob Schrab is a frequent collaborator with Dan Harmon on shows like *Community* (2009-2015) and *Rick & Morty* (2013-present).

One of the best segments in the original *Creepshow* (1982) is "The Crate," which features a grinning beast named Fluffy that looks related to werewolves.

🔘🔘◐⚪

"Fur"
Room 104
Season 4, Episode 11
October 2, 2020

"I've got it, and now I just want to, like, get rid of it or hide it or something."

Set in the era of leg warmers, scrunchies, and synths, two girls sneak into a roadside motel to enjoy their last summer before "it" happens. When a jock swings by and threatens them, the girls transform into werewolves, kick his butt, and celebrate the dude's defeat by singing an original pop anthem called "Fur Sure."

This girl power funfest is written and directed by Mel Eslyn, who frequently collaborates with the Duplass Brothers. She's a co-producer on *Creep 2* (2017) and *The Creep Tapes* (2024-present) about a serial killer who wears a shaggy werewolf mask to embody his terrifying alter ego, Peachfuzz.

🔘🔘🔘🔘

"Shapeshifters Anonymous"
Creepshow
Holiday Special
December 18, 2020

"Your reign of terror ends today, Kringle!"

It's the holiday season, and a man who thinks he's a werewolf goes to a therianthrope support group where he meets a were-cheetah, a were-tortoise, a were-boar, and a furry who's a hippopotamus at heart, and they reveal that Santa Claus is a villain with an age-old vendetta against all shapeshifters.

This episode is written and directed by series creator Greg Nicotero, the legendary SFX and makeup artist whose other werewolf creds include *Ginger Snaps II: Unleashed* (2004), *Ginger Snaps Back: The Beginning* (2004), *Cursed* (2005), and *Hemlock Grove* (2013-2015).

🔘🔘◐⚪

"Blood Moon"
Into the Dark
Season 2, Episode 12
March 26, 2021

"Mom, if I got out, in the house, I mean, you think I'd ever hurt you?"

Strong performances elevate a shaky script in this somber and tense slow burner. Haunted by the memory of her husband's tragic death, Esme is a single mom who moves with her preteen son Luna to a small town in the desert. She homeschools the boy, sheltering him from the world because he's a werewolf who needs to be locked in a cage during every full moon.

Speaking of anthropomorphic animals, episode director Emma Tammi is also behind video game adaptation *Five Nights at Freddy's* (2023) and its upcoming sequels about possessed animatronics at a family pizzeria.

🔘🔘🔘◐

"Mazey Day"
Black Mirror
Season 6, Episode 4
June 15, 2023

"Can't handle the consequences, don't enter the game."

Every so often, *Black Mirror* examines news media, and this time the focus is the dog-eat-dog world of tabloid journalism and the influence of the press on the events they cover. Set in 2006, a young *paparazza* quits after a TV actor she outed takes his own life. When a friend asks her to help find a missing movie star for a hefty reward, they follow the clues to a New Age rehab center and find the young celebrity chained to a bed.

The episode's werewolf was created by British visual effects and computer animation studio Framestore, who previously won Emmys for classic miniseries like *Gulliver's Travels* (1996) and *Merlin* (1998), not to mention Academy Awards for *The Golden Compass* (2007), *Gravity* (2013), and *Blade Runner 2049* (2017).

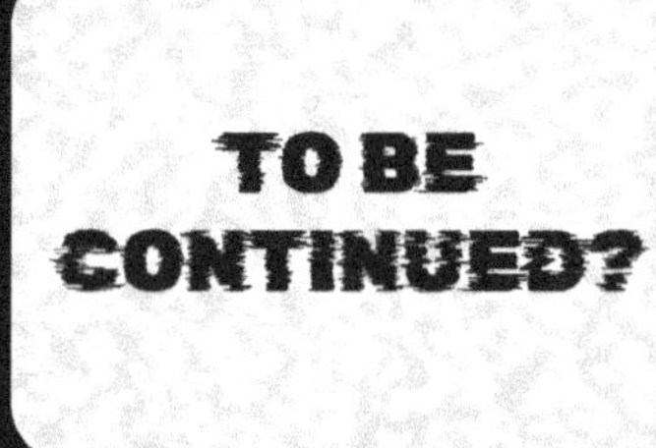

DATE NIGHT
WRITTEN BY K.M. LIGHTFOOT
ART BY JOAQUIN ESPINOSA
28

IT'LL BE LIKE OUR FIRST DATE... AGAIN...
RYAN...
I KNOW. BABY STEPS. IT'S JUST..
IF YOU'RE NOT READY WE CAN PLAN A DIFFERENT NIGHT.
IT'S OK.
CRISTIN, I'VE CHANGED.
I'D LOVE IT IF YOU GAVE ME A CHANCE TO SHOW YOU.
OKAY...
DATE NIGHT

BESIDES...
BUCK MISSES
YOU.

YOU CAN TELL
BUCK I'VE MISSED
HIM TOO.
YEAH.
I'LL
SEE YOU
SOON?

SNAP
SNAP

GOTTA PEE, BUD?
ALRIGHT BE QUICK, IT'S COLD.
TIKTIKTIKTIK

DAMN.

BUCK? I SWEAR IF YOU GET SPRAYED BY A SKUNK AGAIN...
BARK
BARK
BARK

BARK
GRRRAH BARK
BARK
BARK

BARK
BUCK! GET BACK IN HERE!
BARK
BARK

RUUUUAGHH!

OH FUCK—

DATE NIGHT
WRITTEN BY K. M. LIGHTFOOT
ART BY JOAQUÍN ESPINOSA

HNNN

WHAT THE HELL—
—WAS THAT!?

≥GGGAH≥

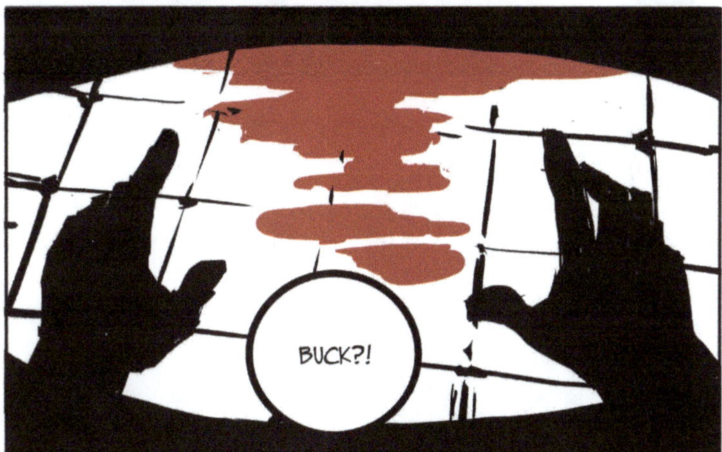

BUCK?!

OH NO—

HNN

IT'S OKAY BUDDY. IT'S OKAY...
HNN
HNNN
HNNN

I'LL VE RIGHT BACK, OKAY?
SHIT.

WHERE THE HELL DID I PUT MY PHONE?!

TSSSSSSS

FU—
—CK!

POP

GGGAH

NNHAAAAH

VZZ
VZZ

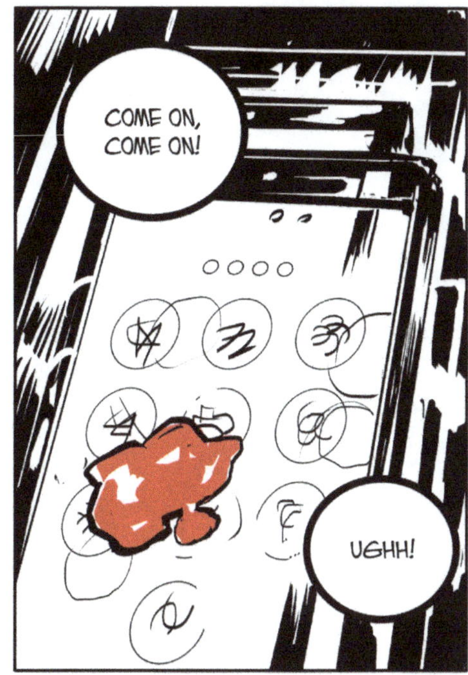

COME ON, COME ON!
UGHH!

CRUNCH

NO...
NO, NO,
NO, NO!

HNN
HNN
HNN
I'M
COMING
BUDDY!

LOOKS LIKE I'LL BE THE ONE SAVING YOU THIS TIME, PAL.
HNN HNN HNN

LET'S GET YOU IN THE CAR.

THIS MIGHT HURT..
SNIFF SNIFF

GRRRR
GRRR
ARGH
BAR AR
R BAR AR

HEY, HEY, IT'S ME.
BARK GRRRK BARK
BUCK, CALM DOWN. IM JUST TRYING TO—

—HELP...

BARGHHKK BARGHK

SHUT THE FUCK UP

SOMETHING IS WRONG...
BARK BARK BARK

WHAT THE HELL IS THE MATTER WITH YOU?
YOU NEED TO TAKE BUCK TO THE HOSPITAL.
YOU NEED TO GO TO THE HOSPITAL.

FUCK... I'M SO HOT.

I CAN'T-

I CAN'T BREATHE.
COUGH
CAN'T-

BREATHE!

-HELP...

MMM...
YOU'VE CHANGED

CRACK
CRACK

GOD PLEASE NO
CRACK
CRACK

NO...

NGGAAHHH

CRUNCH
TINK
TINK
TINK

PLEASE

CRCK
CRCK

FEEL DIZZY...

I FEEL...
CRUNCH

THE CHICKEN...?!

RYAN STOP.

THIS ISN'T YOU.

YOU'VE GOT TO
SHOW CRISTIN

YOU'VE CHANGED

STOP!
GUAHHHHH
CRINK

SSSSSS

KAAAA AAAAPL

IT'S WITH ME AGAIN.
GURAHH
GURAHHHKKK GRUAAHHKKK
RUAAHHKK

THE THING THAT TAKES.

THE THING WANTS EVERY LAST PART OF ME.

GOD, CRISTIN, I WANTED TO SHOW YOU SO BAD.

GAHHROOOO

THAT I'VE BEAT THIS DEMON.
FOR YOU, FOR ME. AND FOR--
BARK
BARK
BARK

OH, BUCK.
GRRRR
YOU'VE SAVED ME SO MANY TIMES.
GRRRR
MY HANDSOME BOY.
IT WANTS YOU...BECAUSE IT KNOWS I LOVE YOU.
IT KNOWS THAT YOU GIVE ME A REASON TO FIGHT.

I PROMISE I FOUGHT, BUDDY.

I FOUGHT...

... UNTIL I COULDN'T.

UH, RYAN,
WHAT THE
HELL – ?

RYAN?!

OH—

GRAUGHHHN

BUCK!

RINGRINGRINGRINGR

GRINGRINGRINGRINGRING

RINGRINGRINGRINGR

WHERE THE FUCK ARE YOU, RYAN?
RINGRINGRINGRING
GRINGRINGRINGRIN
INGRINGRI
GRINGRING
NGRINGRIN
GRINGRING
RINGRINGRINGR
GRINGRINGRING

CALL RYAN!
Calling Ryan...
COME ON!

RING...RING...

PLEASE ANSWER...

RYAN, WHERE ARE YOU?

ALPHAS

By Sera Rae Young

My hands were clasped tightly in front of me, sweat pooling in the space between them. I hated that I was afraid. Fear wasn't going to help me. I needed to control myself, and my breathing. Whatever stupid thing I had done to get here, I'd be able to figure out a way through.

One of the other girls tripped as we came to a standstill, the sound echoed off chamber walls.

"I'm sorry," she whispered and no one answered her.

"Who have you brought to us?" a dull voice whispered.

"Women worthy." A chorus around me spoke as one.

A beat of silence was broken by the lumbering groan of a heavy door opening. What slivers of light leaked through the edges of my blindfold disappeared as I was led into the next room.

"Step up," the one who held my arms commanded me.

I followed the command slowly. The sharp clicks of my heel became an empty thud as the floor changed from solid to hollow. Some sort of platform. At least a few feet high. The fear rose again, in my throat this time. I tried to swallow it.

"Release them." a voice commanded from somewhere in front of me. My hand ties came off, and then my blindfold.

Like graveyard statues in front of us, figures stood in red hooded robes. Each of them with a tall lit candle in their hands.

"Begin," the voice commanded.

Like a possession, the oath left my tongue. A stream of shapeless sounds that I was not permitted to know the meaning of. I only watched the flames. All around me, the words turned into a chant. Then into a song. My voice was not my own.

Though my eyes stayed on the candle flame, I started to see things creeping on the edges of my vision. Shadows and whispers filled the dark room, taking the shape of inky creatures. Surrounding me.

Still speaking the words, I waited for the fear to come again. Instead, my heart raced with something else. Whispers grew into shouts around us. Moans and wails over the steady drone of voices.

The words started making sense. I felt something I'd only glimpsed in flashes my entire life. It howled through me.

Power. Belonging.

Our speech ended and there was silence. I cringed as the lights came up to a beautifully decorated room covered in old photos and rich wood furnishings. The hoods of robes came down and sitting at a claw foot table at the front of the room was the Board.

"Congratulations, you are now a sister in a long line of Sisters of Theta Mu." Kiarra, the sorority president wiped a tear from her eye with a manicured red finger.

"May you always lift her up."

"And hold her hair," cried out Laura sitting just right of Kiarra popping a corked bottle of white grape sparkling cider as the lights came up.

And on the left side of Kiarra, crying as promised, was Georgia with a G.

Moving across the country for college, with no friends, I'd burned myself out on lonely nights eating butter noodles in my dorm room.

My roommate, who I thought would have been an easy first college friend, started seeing a guy who lived off campus after the first month. I saw her maybe three more times that year.

My mom suggested I join a club. Make some friends. Get the real college experience and the most of my state-school tuition. So I braved the beginning of the year mixer my sophomore year.

Everywhere I turned there was a collapsible table, a balloon arch, and a group of smiling people in matching t-shirts. Studying the poster boards from a safe distance, I searched for something that sounded interesting. Or at least might make me interesting. Maybe I'd put off finding myself because there wasn't anything to find. Self-conscious and not paying attention, I'd knocked myself into her while backing away from a man with a ukulele – Georgia with a G.

Georgia was one of those girls with perfect handwriting, matching bedding, and a skin care routine made of tiny beautiful glass bottles. She always smelled amazing. If I hadn't spent almost every second with her for the last month, I'd say she made it look easy. I saw how hard she worked, but she always made time to help people. I think a year ago, I would have hated her. Talked about her to my friends. Called her something small-minded and petty.

Maybe I'd changed, or maybe she was just impossible to hate. She had no fear, no judgement, no limits. To her everything was beautiful, interesting, and going to work out. You couldn't help but feel like it was true when you were with her. After the mixer, it seemed like I was always with her. Somehow, she'd talked me into it.

Two months later, I signed my name into the old tome. Pledged myself to a life as a worthy woman. She was that persuasive. Though her guaranteeing me a sponsored membership was also a huge factor in my decision. We would celebrate tonight with dinner at an Italian restaurant with "the best fettuccine alfredo" and my very first college party hosted by the university's newest fraternity.

In her room, Georgia curled my thick dark hair into soft ripples. In a way that looked like my natural hair, but better. Everything she touched was made better, more as it was meant to be.

"Do you think there will be a lot of people there? With everything going on."

I'd gotten enough texts from my mom about the three students that were attacked last month. Wildfires over the summer pushed wildlife further into town.

Naturally, there'd been more animal sightings than usual. For the most part, casualties had been limited to the garbage bins. Until they found bodies. All of them brothers of one of the oldest fraternities on campus. The popular story was they'd gotten drunk and provoked an animal. People joked about it on socials, but I'd seen the pictures of crying parents at the memorials.

"It's sad, but it was a random animal attack." Georgia sighed, "I'm just worried when they catch the bear they'll… well, you know." She smiled, smoothing my hair and turning off her iron before her face fell again. "Are you worried? We don't have to go."

"I'm going," I replied immediately, "I only joined this thing to go to really cool frat parties and do kegs."

"Oh, me too," Georgia's perfect lips curled at the ends, and my palms were sweaty again.

"Oh, I forgot I got you something shiny!" She twirled around on slippers and ran to pull a velvet box from under her pillow.

"It's tradition," She sat on the bed in matching purple checkered pajamas, looking more excited for the gifts than I was. "Open it."

The little box was heavy. I fumbled with it for a moment, still adjusting to my nails. Fortunately, my hands were sweaty enough they gave me a good grip on the velvet. Inside was a silver necklace with a delicate "N" dangling from it, next to a pair of circular diamond studs.

"This… it's too much…"

"It's moissanite," Georgia shook her head, "but it is real silver."

"I can't accept it,"

"You will," She had a way of rolling her eyes that was somehow loving. "Do you not like it? It's an N… for Nat… should I have done an R? For Renata?."

"No I like it, They are beautiful but I lose these things, that's why I get the cheap stuff." The kind of stuff that leaves green stains all over your skin.

"Well, then don't ever take *these* things off." Georgia stood and pinched the necklace between manicured fingers, "May I?"

I nodded, helpless to refuse her. She stepped around me, hands draping the necklace around my neck to clasp it. Her hands rested on my shoulders, pulling me to look in the mirror.

"See, a perfect fit." Her hands trailed on my collarbone. She looked me up and down from my shoulder, and I swallowed.

Georgia could make time move in slow motion. That's how it felt, when she watched me. My heart beat so loud I was afraid she could hear it, with how close she was. Finally, her eyes met mine and she smiled again. All straight white teeth.

"The Beta boys are gonna die when they see you tonight."

"Wanna come over to the dark side?" Imani swiped her ring finger into her pot of glitter and brushed it lightly on my cheek.

"Sorry?" I'd gotten distracted watching KJ and Paula roll a "girl blunt" on a metallic purple tray. Music from the party thudded like one never-ending song outside the door.

"Art History…" Imani was intensely feminine. Like a doe -eyed doll straight out of the meadows they filmed perfume commercials in. "I was a comms major, but I took an Occult Art History class my first semester for fun and I loved it."

"I need to do that more. I've just been taking my gen eds…" I was comfortable with the girls, but some part of me still thought I needed to distract them from how boring and unlike them I was. "So you probably like scary movies."

"As much as anyone does, I'm more interested in the real stuff." She twisted the silver cap onto her pot and slipped it into her tiny purse.

"Like what?"

"Every scary story has a little bit of truth to it, the same as any legend," Imani leaned in and the glitter on her cheeks sparkled. "Sometimes it's a warning, or a secret…" Her lips parted to continue just as KJ and Paula cheered.

"I did it!" KJ held a tiny roll in her fingers.

"You did so good," Paula smiled proudly from the edge of the bath tub, before getting serious. "Wait, is anyone allergic to calendula, or lavender, or mint?"

"I don't think so," I'd look up calendula later.

"Okay great," Paula pulled out a bedazzled lighter and lit the end, breathing in slowly before offering it to me. "Oh… also this has weed in it."

"Yea, I got that." I shook my head. I'd never done it before. Not because I didn't want to, but because no one had offered. Paula didn't need to know that though.

"Alright alright, you never know." Paula waved her hands apologetically.

I inhaled, and silently prayed I wouldn't cough. I tasted the mint, cool smoke entered my mouth and I let it sit before letting it out again.

"Woah big one," Imani nodded, watching me suspiciously.

"You've never done that before in your life have you?" Paula asked after a beat.

I shook my head and felt the betrayal of a tickle in my throat. A violent cough erupted from my core. Desperate, I grabbed onto the empty towel rack for support. I felt my balance flip as the cheap fixture broke off the wall. Paula caught me, struggling to support me as the tears fell from her laughing eyes. There was a another scream as she slipped from my weight and we both fell into the bathtub. KJ and Imani gasped between genuine concerns of "are", "you", and "okay?" My ribs hurt, but I was too disoriented to care. I swallowed trying to control myself until my deep breaths turned into laughter as well. A giant sticker covered water bottle appeared before me, held tenderly by KJ for me to drink from while Paula held my head in caring hands.

"Well, did you like it?" Paula wiped a tear from my eye and then her own.

"Yea, why?" I swallowed again.

"Good." Paula kissed the top of my head. My face felt stretched and tired from laughing and coughing but I felt strangely comfortable sprawled in a bathtub with my legs in the air.

"Wait, let's take a picture in the bathtub?" KJ jumped up with her phone, setting it on the counter to face me, "I used to do it with my friends back home at every party. It's cute, I swear."

I made eye contact with Imani, who shrugged and checked herself in the mirror one last time.

"Alright, but if any of my skin makes direct contact with these surfaces I'm gonna scream." She climbed in around Paula and I as KJ set the self timer, before running to join us in the tub. The flash went off and I didn't need to remember to smile.

"Are my Theta Mu's having a good time?" A soccer tee appeared from behind them, shouting over the music. His sandy hair peaking out from beneath the band of a backwards hat. We'd come from the bathroom to join the rest of the girls in the living room for dancing.

"The music's bad," Jorgia with a J crossed her arms.

I laughed, Georgia flashed her eyes at me and grabbed my hand to lead me into the kitchen.

It was brightly lit and well stocked with alcohol and whey protein. A girl I didn't recognize was sweating over the counter, in a graveyard of jello shots.

"Hey girl," Georgia went straight for her, but gestured with her eyes for me to grab water. "How are we feeling?"

"I'm sorry," I heard the girl whisper. I rinsed a solo cup and filled it from the tap, knowing any sort of filter in this house was probably far past its time.

"Here," I took the hand she gripped on the counter and lifted it with her to her mouth. "It's just water."

"Thank you," she smiled up at me, her eyes were glassy and tearing. I looked at Georgia who seemed equal parts amused and concerned. Then the girl twitched, her body curled up and her hand went straight up to her mouth, spilling all of the water.

"Okay," Georgia lifted the girl in her arms, "we're going outside."

"I'm gonna walk her home," Georgia pulled Alyssa up from where she kneeled, "You're on the other side of the river right?"

"Yea," Alyssa wiped her mouth with the back of her hand.

"Wait," I felt my heart sputter, "you shouldn't walk."

"If I call a car she's gonna hurl in it, and I can't drive so we're walking. Really, I don't mind."

"No I mean, what about the… bear."

I'd never seen Georgia confused before, but she looked almost frustrated.

"The attacks." I repeated.

"Oh," Georgia laughed, "I'm not worried about it, I promise I'll be safe."

"I can come with you," I insisted.

"No, you should keep an eye on the girls. I'll call a car when I drop her off."

"Okay," I looked at my feet in the mud. It was like when Georgia asked me to do something I had to. "Text me when you get there and send me your ride tracker thing."

"Ride tracker thing, got it."

They walked off and Alyssa waved. It seemed like a good sign. Though my mind was racing with all the terrible things that could happen to two girls walking at night.

I felt someone watching me and turned to see the door guy sitting on the front porch step.

"You're one of the new Theta Mu's right?" His arms were wrapped around his sides. His breath made clouds in the night air.

"Yea," I looked into the windows of the house flashing with lights and thrumming admittedly better music. "Are you one of the new Betas?"

"Not yet, technically…" I must have made a face because he added , "I know… alright, you don't need to feel bad. They're just using me but I think I can get a bid out of it by next semester."

"I hope you do."

"I'm not proud of it, but I don't know, I'm just trying to get the full experience."

"I actually do get that."

"My friend from high school says rushing is like buying friends."

"Maybe."

He laughed at that, and I unfortunately felt bad for him. I'd felt like him just a few months ago. With no one to talk to but my mom. He obviously wanted to talk to *someone*. Philanthropy was a part of the code of worthy women…

"I think it's been different than I thought it would be," I'd taken a seat on the step above him, "it's about finding the right group, just like anything." He'd told me about his family, his friends, and his fear of fish. Everything.

"You think Beta's not for me?"

"I do not know you."

He looked at me and smiled like a little boy.

"I'm Pete." He shook his head, "and that girl was the frat sweetheart. Which really just means most of the guys hook up with her and she brings pizza rolls to parties." He took a sip of his own beer. "Frat sweethearts should be more girls like you." He looked at me, the lights from inside strobing in his dark eyes. He leaned in and before I knew what was happening his lips were on mine. I pushed him back, slowly wincing, hoping I'd let him off the hook by being gentle about it.

"I need to find my friends," I started to get up and he grabbed my hand.

"Just cause I'm not a member?"

"No…" I pulled away, his grip wasn't hard but it wasn't welcome.

"Well I actually can't let you in, we're at capacity… fire code, you understand," he looked to the front door and shrugged.

I rolled my eyes. Bad jokes and bad timing didn't warrant a mercy chuckle. My heart started thundering and I walked around the side of the house to the back door.

"Hey, I was joking okay, just wait…" I heard him following.

I tried not to run, he grabbed my hand again turning me towards him.

"I'm not like, gonna make you do anything, okay?"

"Okay then let me go inside to my friends."

"I will alright, I'm not that guy."

"Then let me in." My voice was getting louder, shrill. Fear simmered under every inch of my skin.

"Promise you won't say anything…"

"No," I shoved him away and realized I'd let him back me up into the tree line. His dark eyes grew wilder. He was standing wide so I couldn't run past him.

"Calm – " Pete snapped, before turning his head to the house and lowering his voice to a whisper "Just promise me, you'll…"

The sound rumbled from the earth. Bringing my unsure steps to a halt. Hollow and hoarse, something massive and hungry. Coming from behind me. The full moon escaped through barren tree tops littering the forest floor in lacy shadows. I couldn't tell which was my own. A strange gaze lingered on my exposed back. It felt curious, waiting. I turned slowly, trying to remember how to breathe. A mouth opened up before me. Thick branches and briars circled like teeth. The darkness was breathing.

Messes of autumn leaves, glowing purple in the moonlight, crunched as whatever stood before me inched closer. The gentle give and the growing sound of haggard breath felt like hands grasping me by the shoulders. I needed to run, I needed to scream, I needed to – before I could finish my thought, it stepped forward into a thin band of blue, and I saw the face of midnight.

I heard Pete curse and run off behind me.

The creature was terrifying, inhuman, and somehow beautiful. It studied me as I studied it, and then it backed away into the darkness again.

I blinked, my heart returning to a semi-normal rhythm and I saw a figure emerge from the darkness again, in a torn white dress.

"Are you okay?" Georgia with a G said with no respect for my ruined reality. She grabbed me in her arms, starkly warm against the cool autumn night. "I know you have a lot of questions. We're supposed to answer them at the sleepover tomorrow. Just…" She pulled away and put her hands on each side of my face, eyes wide, "did I scare you?"

"No." I said, without hesitation, my thoughts so scattered I couldn't muster anything else. After a long moment, we both laughed.

"Does it hurt?" We walked through the woods along the river. Georgia walked in front of me, wearing my sweater.

"Yes," Georgia sighed, "but only for a second."

"And I do that too?" I was still unsure of what to call it.

"Eventually, if you want to," She looked back at me, asking a question of her own.

"What about…" I paused… *the animal attacks, those students, their parents.*

Georgia seemed to sense it. I'd never seen her look afraid, but she did for a moment. I realized she was afraid of what I might think of her. Of the sisterhood. There were questions I couldn't ask yet. I wasn't ready for things to change. All I could think of was how beautiful and quiet everything was. I'd never walked at night like this. Just me and another girl. That question could wait.

"What about Pete?"

"Pete, huh?" She looked up at the moon, smiling only with her mouth, before turning to wink at me.

"No one's ever gonna believe him."

The Locket

Written by
K.M. Lightfoot

Art by
Jesuza Diaz

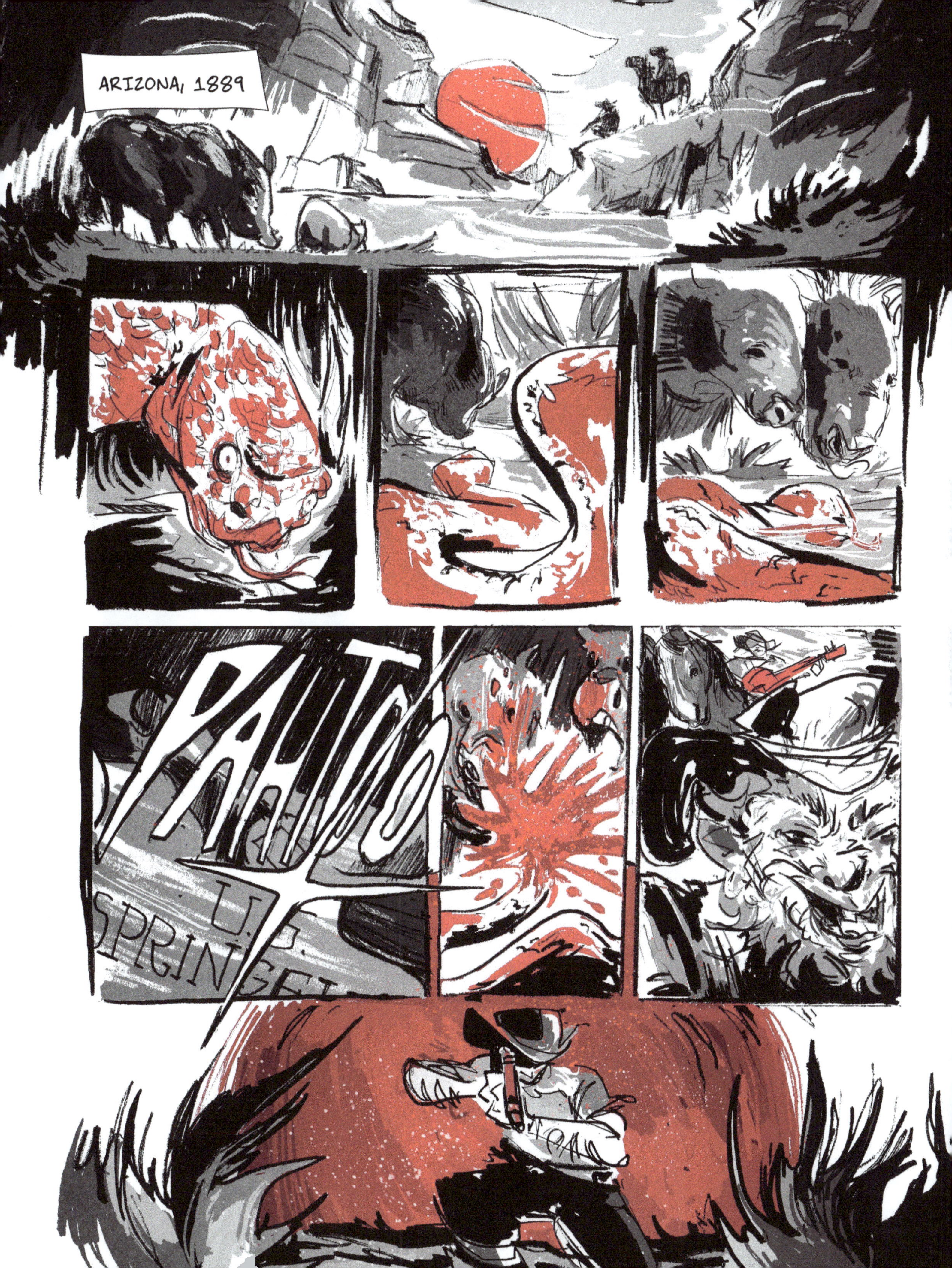

ARIZONA, 1889

THE LOCKET
WRITTEN BY
K.M. LIGHTFOOT
ART & LETTERING BY
JESUZA DÍAZ

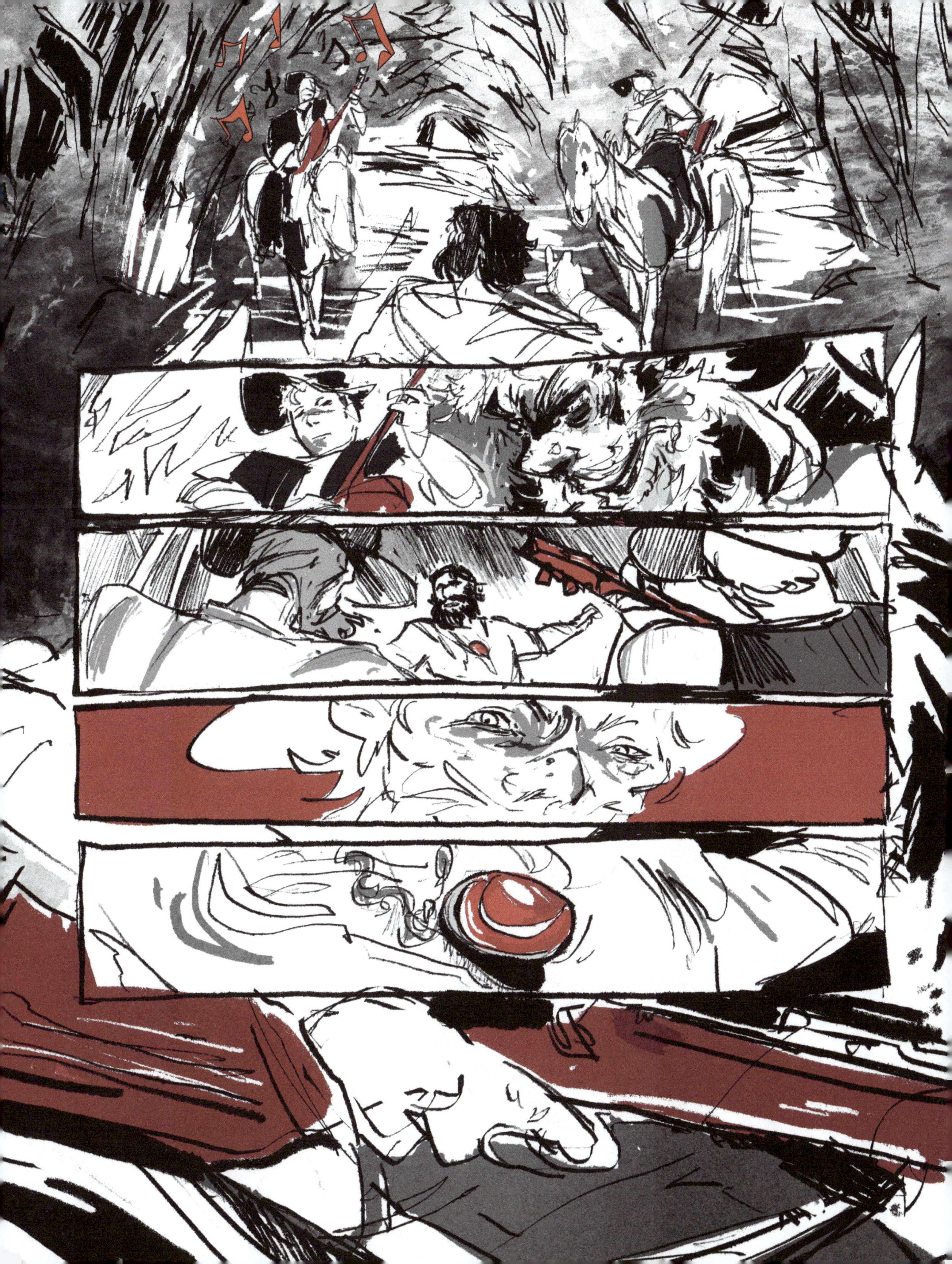

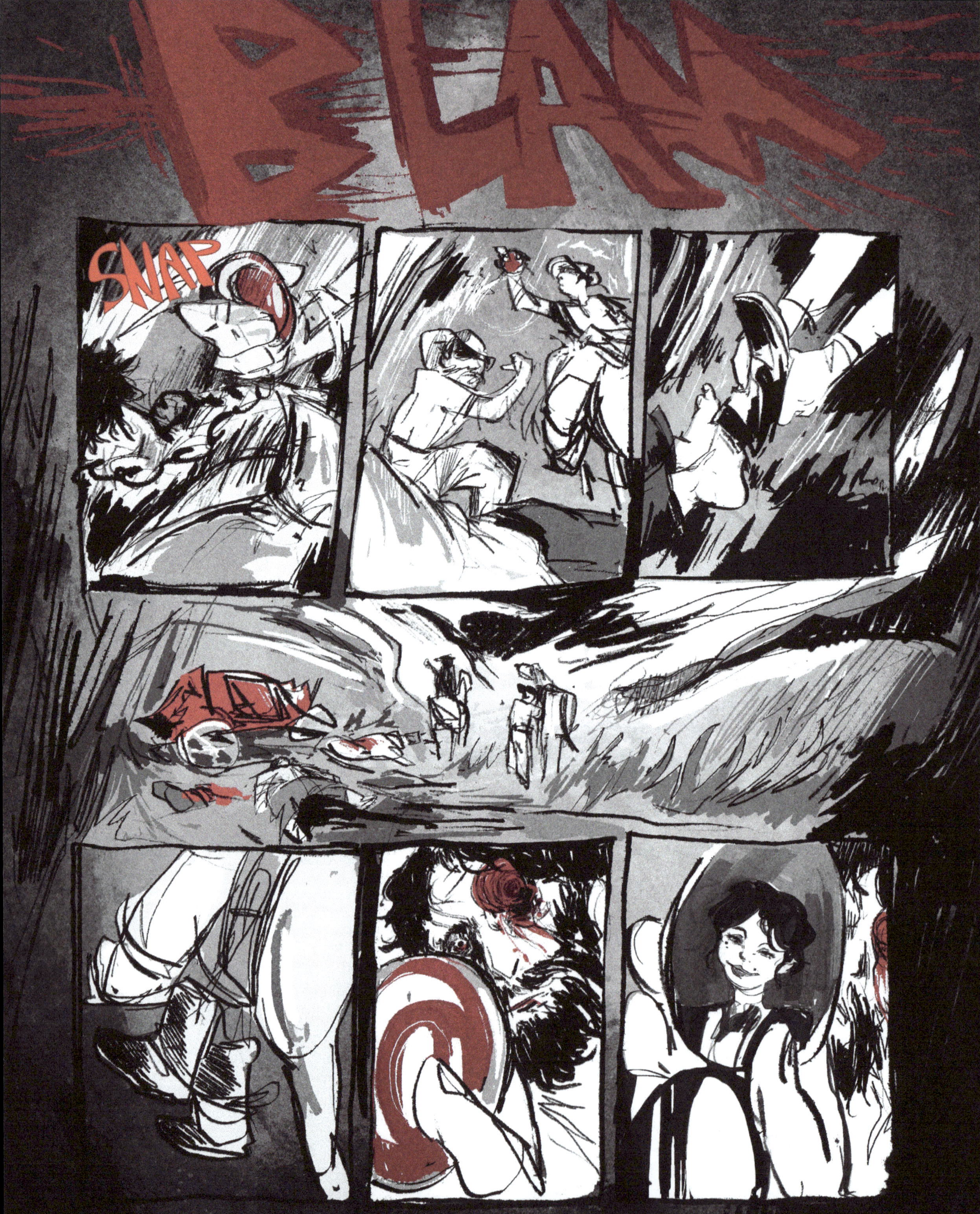
BLAM
SNAP

ENGLAND 1886

CRUNCH

GROWLING

HUFF
HUFF

DR. THOM
DR. WILLIAMS
DR. SMITH
DR. TOPH
DR. WILLER
DR. HEFFCUR
DR. EARNSHAW
EXPLORE THE MYSTERY OF THE AMERICAN WEST
Home of NAVAJO and their enigmatic healers, the Haatali!

SNIFF
SNIFF

CRAK

SNAP

THE STORY OF "REMAINS"

By Nicholas Aaron Hodge

Stories are eternal. They persist. Even if the body dies, the soul of a story will soon find itself rising again in an entirely new form.

Understanding this mutable nature has always been a key component for me in truly appreciating the art of storytelling. In order to tell a good story, a curious mind should research and discover the many diverse kinds of stories that have already been told and most essentially, why they were told.

A journey of discovery which is not nearly as easy as it sounds, especially in the case of stories from cultures far removed from your own that have been systematically erased, oppressed, or simply forgotten.

However, I believe that it is the responsibility of any conscientious and empathetic person to seek out, uncover, and engage with the history and beliefs of cultures such as this in order to gain a better understanding of the greater story of humanity that we all share at the very least. It is precisely this pursuit that led to the creation of this story I have called, "Remains"

Back in 2021, Kaleb and I began talking about a film concept (as we often do) set in the familiar environs of Chicago's northern suburban edge on the fateful night that a Werewolf washes up on shore and proceeds to wreak wanton havoc. At its core, this pitch was an attempt to deliver the kind of bold, big spectacle, genre fiction attached to big cities like New York and L.A. to the city we know and call home. Additionally, we were attempting to envision the most surprising threat that could befall the windy city,

"Aliens?"

"No, that's kinda been done."

"Vampires?"

"Too believable- they'd blend in."

"What about a Werewolf?"

"Now that is interesting..."

While we never actually got around to finishing a draft of that story, the unique imagery, alluring mystery, and imaginative potential of this half-formed idea remained embedded in our minds for years and is certainly a contributing factor to the creation of the book you are holding in your hands right now.

So, when we inevitably settled on the subject of "Werewolves" for our horror anthology, the pervading question became, "What kinds of Werewolf stories would we want to read?"

In my case, I found myself drawn back to that screenplay idea from years ago, as I pondered the origins of our titular Lake Michigan bound Werewolf.

"Where had it come from? Who was the host of the beast? How long had it been in the water? Did it come from an island up north? Or perhaps it floated all the way from Michigan across the bay?"

The mystery only deepened.

This notion was only further articulated as I found myself reflecting on the popular Werewolf media I love, and realized that the origins of the Werewolf are rarely given credence. More often than not, a protagonist in a Werewolf tale is bitten by a random, already existent Werewolf, thereby perpetuating a curse of bad luck and bad timing more than the iconic lunar aversion and iconic transformation.

The Fountain, No. 1:
"The Wounded Indian
Slaking His Death Thirst"
Thomas Cole 1843

Around the same time, I happened to attend an exhibition at the historic Newberry Library in downtown Chicago, which concerned the Indigenous peoples of Illinois and their history in the region. The notion of the ancient lands of Illinois, long before the sprawling concrete monolith of Chicago was ever conceived, has fascinated me ever since I moved to the city nearly a decade ago. This interest has only further compounded in subsequent years as I have learned about ancient trade roads in the region and the tragically destroyed earthwork burial mounds of numerous Native American cultures nearby in Ohio.

One of the books on display at this exhibition was a collection of Indigenous Anishinaabe folk tales published by Michigan State University Press and written and edited by Howard Webkamigad entitled, Ottawa Stories From the Springs. This book is an invaluable collection of traditional stories that have been collected and documented via recorded interviews with Anishinaabe leaders and even written in the Anishinaabe language. For clarification, the word "Anishinaabe" is the regional moniker for the founding tribes of the Ojibwe, Odawa, Potawatomi, Algonquin, Nipissing, Mississaugas, Oji-Cree, and Chippewa (Saulteaux).

As I studied these literary accounts, I was shocked to discover one specific tale that seemed to eerily align with the framing of my own developing story. This story is entitled, "The Story of the Young Anishinaabe Woman and Her Dog."

Like many of the stories in this anthology, the explicit meaning of this tale in the context of its original telling is lost. However, the function of this story as a moral tale meant to impart a lesson to the listener is very much still intact.

In this story, we learn that it was a custom of the Anishinaabe people long ago to send young people coming of age out into the wilderness for ten days in order to "seek their vision" in a sacred place. The focus of our story, the titular "Young Anishinaabe Woman," goes on her journey with her faithful dog and returns after ten days with a plot to leave her family once and for all.

Over some time, the Young Woman stores enough supplies for her journey and departs into the wilderness, never to be seen by her community ever again. Years later, a traveling group of Anishinaabe warriors discover the missing Young Girl inhabiting the "Spirit Islands" of northern Lake Michigan, bizarrely having married her Dog and given birth to Human/Dog hybrid children. So, the warriors travel home and tell the Woman's older brother about their horrifying discovery, and he returns to the island with a new group of warriors and kills her and her family, declaring that from then on, no Anishinaabe shall ever have such a union with a beast.

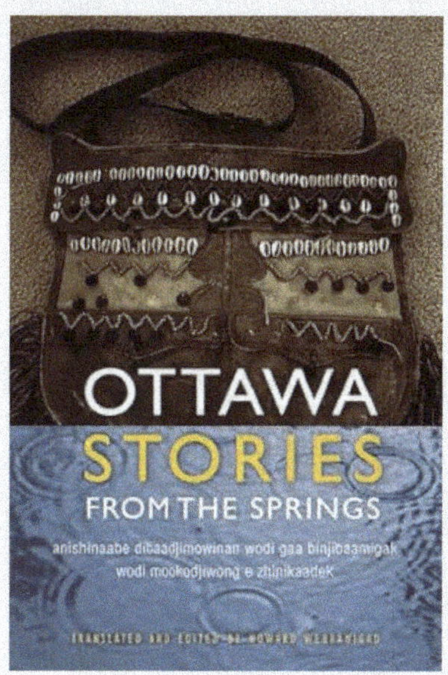

Ottawa Stories From the Springs
by Howard Webkamigad

It was all there. The island. The wolf (well, a dog, but it's close). A connection to a story that speaks far beyond the trifling spectacle of the modern world. In discovering this story, passed down through time, I realized that I had an opportunity to infuse my story with something timeless and poignant. Rather than a story focused primarily on the Werewolf, "Remains" became much more concerned with the character and inner life of the "Young Anishinaabe Woman," who I have called "Baswewe" after the Anishinaabe word for "echo/echo maker."

While the final product is admittedly a piece of genre fiction of the Horror variety (this is a horror anthology after all), I hope that I have equally expressed elements of the tragic, forgotten history of the Anishinaabe people from which this tale feels so naturally derived. I hope that in reading this new account, you are encouraged to learn more about the diverse Anishinaabe people, or even feel compelled to explore the lands they once called home. Lastly, I hope that "Remains" can be a continued reminder that we must not forget, abandon, or erase our history no matter how painful.

-Nicholas Aaron Hodge

Nakweshkodaadidaa ekobiiyang
(Let's meet by the water)
Giwaabamaanaan maashkinewaabikizid
dibiki-giizis
(We all see her the full shaped moon)
Apiichi bagosendamang
(While we all have hope)

Remains

Written by
Nicholas Aaron Hodge

Art & Lettering by
Renato Zechetto

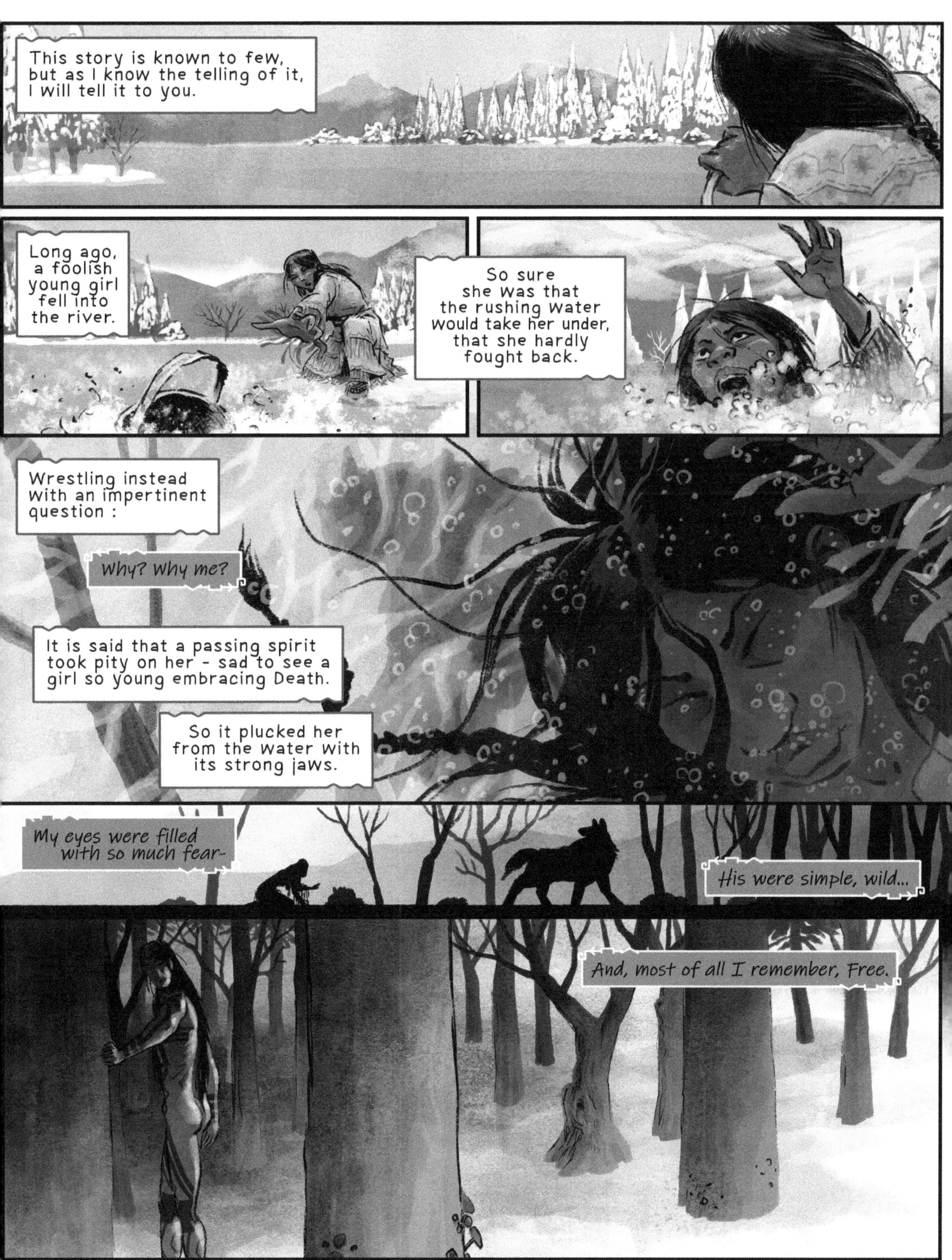

This story is known to few, but as I know the telling of it, I will tell it to you.

Long ago, a foolish young girl fell into the river.

So sure she was that the rushing water would take her under, that she hardly fought back.

Wrestling instead with an impertinent question :

Why? Why me?

It is said that a passing spirit took pity on her - sad to see a girl so young embracing Death.

So it plucked her from the water with its strong jaws.

My eyes were filled with so much fear-

His were simple, wild...

And, most of all I remember, Free.

Curious it was, that the girl should feel so frustrated with the gift of life.
Haunted as she was by the memory of the man who was also a wolf.
She made a promise to herself that should she ever cross paths with the spirit again-
she would be ready.
Yet somehow, he knew.
Wordlessly, he knew what I would ask of him. His eyes returning a question of his own.
"ARE YOU SURE?"

But the girl did not waver in her request.
longing for something beyond her understanding.
A different kind of life.
Her and the Wolf Man—
and the unknown.

That should be the end of her story, should it not?
REMAINS
ART & LETTERING RENATO ZECHETT
PART OF THE WEREWOLF LIVES! ANTHOLOGY
BY NICHOLAS AARON HODGE
If only it were so easy for man.
To cease his endless searching for answers.
To accept what he does not understand.
MA IINGANAG...
To loosen his grip on the past.

There was so much I didn't yet understand...
Blinded as I was by freedom in those early days of flight.
I had given so much of myself away...
Did I even recognize what was left?
The girl made a new vow-
to protect herself and the one's she loved-
and cease her wild raging.

She would find contentment in the dream of a home.
A life that would no longer be her own

And for the first time in either of their lives—
all of it was enough.
And the hunger that lived deep inside of her—
crying out to be free—
became sated at last by something simple called, love.
BASWEWE, MY LOVE. RETURN TO US!
For what else should she need?

The Wolf Man had told her only as much as she needed to know about the change-
that it would hurt, that it would last many moons.
But when their sons came into the world-
the Wolf Man changed into something new-
a Father.
He told them much about his people, far more ancient than her own, revealing secret teachings in the stars.
And when the Moon called, the Father and his Sons would shed their false skin together-
as once she had, but would no longer.
And deep within herself, a small seed of regret began to grow...

She too became something else in those days.
A ghost.
Though she was never really alone.
Some days she foolishly wondered—
"Is this life anything like the one I wished for?"
She learned then that wishes are much like curses—
they could change as frighteningly as she could.

She had spent so much time desiring to live in some pleasant future—
only to then find herself confronted with the past.
SISTER, DON'T YOU REMEMBER ME? WE SEARCHED FOR SO LONG... BUT I NEVER GAVE UP HOPE.
What had her life become—
but a festering wound?
RETURN WITH ME. BE WHERE YOU BELONG.
One that gets worse with the scratching—
and will never fully heal.

I remember feeling proud as I paddled, knowing for the first time, that no man-
no matter how strong, could ever hope to possess something as untamable as me or my spirit.
Only to find that while I wasn't looking- my heart had been taken-
leaving behind nothing at all-
not even the memory of a heart.

In her long life, she had learned much about the natural world to which she belonged—
Of Life—
Of Love—
Of Death, too.
She thought to educate these men about the latter—
over and over again until the knowledge of it stuck.

Why is it that men such as these.
Those who would take the whole world by the handful-
-think that any God is watching over them?
GNAHR!!!
After all-

Your God left you here with me-
-and I am always hungry.

That should be the end of her story, should it not?
Once she was no one-
-until she became a Memory-
-then a Mother-
-and now a Beast.
She did not want to know what she would become next.

How?
How could she live when they did not?
She would not leave her family again.
The island would be her tomb too.
And if any other man should come here-
they would share it.

And with no one to remember my name-
I embraced the change like a new lover-
-and I forgot my pain.
She forgot herself-
and at last, she was finally free.
But after awakening from such an endless, empty dream-
-why did the hurt still remain ?

In spite of it all, for the first time in an age—
she dared imagine a life for herself—
A different kind of life.
The kind man tried his best to communicate,—
and slowly she began to understand—
The long months of the changing had stretched to years—
-the world had gone on without her and her hunger had let it.
And the little that was left of the girl ached to hear of what she had done.

So she made a new vow-
to use the remnants of her pain to rebuild. To finally leave this place behind.
Maybe now-
after all this time-
she would start to mend all that had been broken.
I could learn what it meant to be whole again-

-but only if she let me.

Had she not fed long enough on her grief?

For the first time in a long time- her only wish was to remain herself.

Surely there was still something resembling love left within her...

Baswewe...

say your name...

let her hear you

...

But if there was one thing she knew above all else—
Pain grows stronger the longer it is allowed to live.
It grows roots.
It swallows you whole.
It too changes—
and just when you think it's gone?

It comes back.
...NAKWESHKODAADIDAA EKOBIIYANG...
Why should a thing like me be free?
I never meant for my life to be like this...
...GIWAABAMAANAAN MAASHKINEWAABIKIZID DIBIKI-GIIZIS...
If I could go back- only for a moment- things could be so different. I could be whole again...
...APIICHI BAGOSENDAMANG!
MOTHER! KEEP UP!
SHE'LL KILL US ALL!
RUN! IT'S HER, IT'S THE MONSTER!
If I could hold them one last time- If I could tell them to run-

If I had never come here-

...what then?
You... this is all your fault!

You tricked me- You stole me- You gave me this life without telling me how to live!

You left me ALONE!
THERE! DO YOU SEE! BEHOLD THE BEAST!
HELP US!
PLEASE DON'T HURT ME- NOT AGAIN!
That should be the end of her story, should it not?

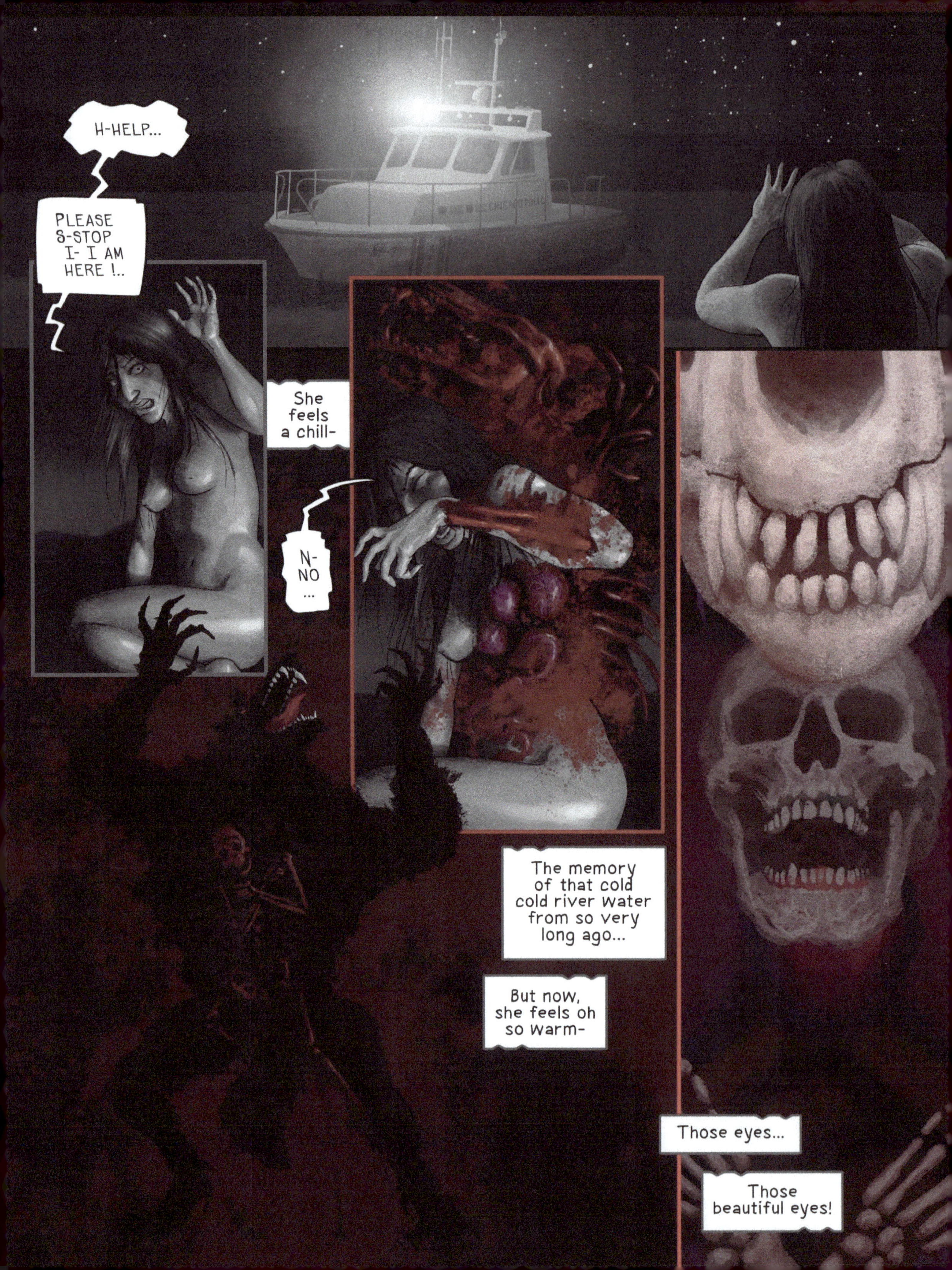

H-HELP...
PLEASE S-STOP I- I AM HERE !..
She feels a chill-
N-NO ...
The memory of that cold cold river water from so very long ago...
But now, she feels oh so warm-
Those eyes...
Those beautiful eyes!

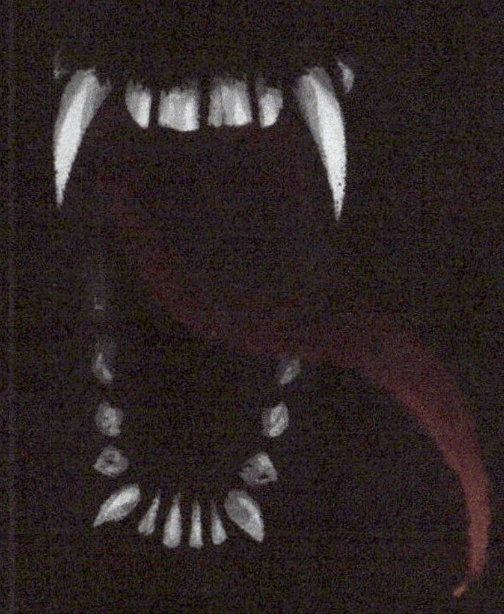

TO BE
CONTINUED
IN

"WOLFMAN
TAKES CHICAGO!"

What is the best Werewolf Movie of All Time?

Werewolf fans are the best. They're unwavering, passionate and hot. That's not an opinion, it's fact. When you ask someone, "Would you be a werewolf or a vampire?" The werewolf crowd doesn't hesitate to show their loyalty. We all stand strong in our kinship for the midnight beast...

... until you ask us "What is the Best Werewolf Movie of All Time?"

The popularity of the werewolf owes an abundance of its enduring and iconic qualities to cinematic interpretations. The involuntary transformation during a full moon, passing the curse through biting others, and a relentless desire to conduct a murder spree on fellow humans were all emboldened on the big screen. These traits helped define and provide guidelines for the hairy crown jewel in the modern monster pantheon.

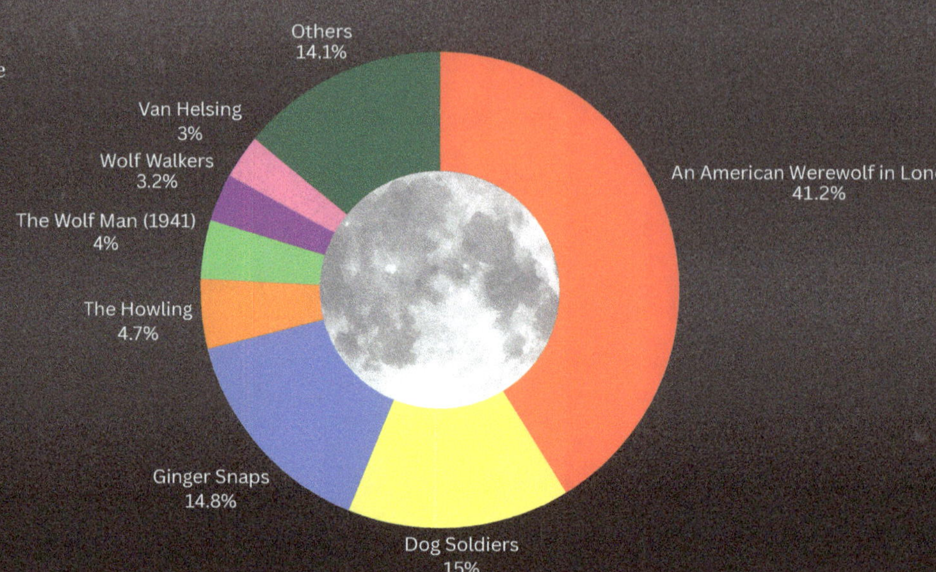

When making a compendium of all things werewolf, leaving out a fundamental medium of the mythos seemed... dangerous. This led Nick and I to find a way to include an interactive component of marketing to generate interest in the book.

Over several months we posted on various social media platforms, subreddits, and even held polls at the world renowned Music Box Theatre in Chicago to collect data. With over a 1000 votes, we finally have an answer!

We started the poll with the six movies we believed to be the "heavy hitters" of the werewolf zeitgeist: *An American Werewolf in London, Ginger Snaps, The Wolf Man (1941), The Howling, The Silver Bullet,* and *Dog Soldiers.* We allowed our participants to vote for the initial six, or to vote for their unlisted choice in the "other" section which we'd then add to the next round of polling. By the time we wrapped up our final polling, our selection of movies grew to twenty two!

The most fascinating race was for spots #2 and #3. *Ginger Snaps, The Wolf Man,* and *Teen Wolf,* began with strong silver and bronze numbers which changed as frequently and willing as the werewolves of the *Underworld* franchise.

I was surprised to see *The Wolf Man* (1941), the film that popularized the creature, fall off after the third poll. Not a single person voted for it in three polls. Heartbreaking. The film did rally towards the end securing the 5th spot overall.

I initially undervalued the power of *Teen Wolf* as it polled alongside *An American Werewolf in London* for the first few weeks before limping off the court, but hey, it was rebooted as a pretty successful TV show in 2011, or so I hear.

A pair of late inclusions, *Wolf Walkers,* an animated film from 2020, and the controversial *Van Helsing* from 2004 (which has some of my favorite werewolf designs put on screen) were polling high and consistent. They just suffered from being added late into the poll process to change their werewolf film placement destiny.

While the ebb and flow with new choices kept things changing, it was pretty clear *An American Werewolf in London* was walking away with the title. Meanwhile the *Dog Soldiers* and *Ginger Snaps* were fighting tooth and claw for second place. It wasn't clear until the very last poll which of the two films would be taking the second place spot. In the end, by one singular vote, *Dog Soldiers* was victorious over *Ginger Snaps* securing the #2 spot.

Yet, with all the drama behind the race for silver, it was still abundantly clear who was going to be the champion.

With 41% of the overall votes *An American Werewolf in London* howled past any competition. Each week I saw it completely overtake any challenger. It made me question why this film has become the seminal werewolf film of our age? So I rewatched it.

And I felt the same way I did on first viewing...elated. It's hilarious. It's smart with its horror, exploring the subconscious terror specifically designed to frighten the young Jewish American college graduate protagonist. It's sexy, David Naughton and Jenny Agutter are breaking the thermostat here! That transformation scene is STILL the transformation scene to beat for any new werewolf project. It proved that the Werewolf is a story telling vehicle with plenty of gas left in the tank!

-K.M. Lightfoot

Continued on the next page!

www.ingramcontent.com/pod-product-compliance
Lightning Source LLC
Chambersburg PA
CBHW041211100726
47911CB00017B/921